JOURNEY

OF THE

SHEPHERD WOMAN

REMARKABLE WOMEN OF THE BIBLE

BY

Carlene Havel

and

Sharon Faucheux

Cover design by Bespoke.com

Quotes are taken from the King James version of the Bible

Contents

Chapter One

John Simon placed his clothing on the table where a soldier sat writing. Knowing it was futile to attempt to hide anything, he laid the leather pouch full of coins in full view on top of his garments.

The gray-haired Roman scribe laid his reed pen aside to examine the purse. When the pouch was emptied, he grunted and tossed it aside, leaving the coins stacked in front of him.

"Full name?"

"John Simon, sir."

"Occupation?"

"I am a shepherd in the hill country near here. I came into the city this morning, planning to return to the hills by evening."

"What is your connection to this rabble? Are you their leader?" The old soldier waved a beefy hand toward the line of naked men whose names he had already recorded.

"I do not know these men. I was walking down the street when I turned a corner and found myself in the midst of a riot."

"Of course you did." The old soldier chuckled. "And no doubt you love everything Roman and swear absolute allegiance to Caesar." He turned and let his eyes slowly travel the full length of John Simon's nude body. "Well, what have we here? You have not been circumcised," he said, with obvious surprise. "Therefore, you cannot possibly be one of these Jews. Where are you from? What nationality are you?"

"I was raised in Ephesus by a Jewish mother. My father was Greek. He served in the Roman army for many years."

The soldier held his pen poised in midair. "Name?"

A guard poked his head inside the shelter. "The lictors are ready for another prisoner."

The soldier at the table pointed to the slender man at the end of the line. "You. Go." As the naked man followed the guard outside, the recorder barked, "Well?"

"Johannus Simonus." John Simon replied, this time using the Roman pronunciation.

"Not your name, fool. Your father's."

"Linus Simonus," John Simon replied, only belatedly remembering to add, "Sir." He struggled to block out the screams that resounded from the adjacent courtyard. Although he dreaded a Roman beating, he believed he could endure it. He suspected some of the emaciated men in line ahead of him would not survive the lictors' whips.

The old soldier stood and faced John Simon, so close their noses almost touched. After a long stare, he spoke. "Yes, I do see Linus Simonus in your face, even though you do not have his fair hair." He rubbed his chin. "Put on your clothes and wait outside, over there." He jerked a thumb toward a corner of the shelter.

John Simon quickly obeyed, confused but hopeful he might somehow be spared a dreadful scourging. He hurried out of the hut and flattened himself against the rough wooden planks of the hut's wall, standing perfectly still and trying not to call attention to himself in any way. From where he stood, he could not see the punishment taking place, for which he was more than grateful. The cries and moans of the victims were enough to make him cringe.

After what seemed to be a long time, the gray-haired soldier came and took John Simon's arm. "Come with me." As they walked toward the gate of the military compound, he said, “I am Marius Secundus. Your father and I served together.”

“I hardly knew him,” John Simon confessed. “He was killed when I was not quite five years old.”

“I know.” Secundus opened the gate, grunted at the guards, and led John Simon into the street. “I was there.” After they walked a short distance in silence, he stopped. “Your father was a brave man and a good friend. He lost his life saving mine. Now, finally, I have repaid the debt I owe him.” Secundus handed John Simon his empty purse. “Your coins helped persuade the centurion you should be let go.”

John Simon tucked the flattened pouch into his belt. “Truly, I was not involved in the riot.”

“Whether you were or were not makes no difference. Go on your way, and take care you do not get into trouble again. The next time you show up at the barracks, I will not be able to help you.” The old soldier walked away swiftly.

John Simon hurried through the empty streets, shaken by his narrow escape. He came to Jerusalem to contribute to the upkeep of widows and orphans supported by the disciples. Now, his only wish was to get home. The lengthening shadows reminded him to hasten before the city gates were shut for the night.

As soon as he was outside the city walls, John Simon cast about for a makeshift weapon. He lost his shepherd’s rod when the Roman soldiers herded him in with the rioters. Then, he had discretely let his knife drop into the street, not wanting to be armed when he was taken into custody. After selecting a few smooth stones and placing them into his empty coin pouch, John Simon veered off the road. He knew the hills well enough to find his way home in the dark. He preferred meeting a wild animal to risking an encounter with the bandits who sometimes roamed the roads at night.

After the last of the twilight faded, a three-quarter moon rose to guide his steps as he navigated the rough terrain.

Chapter Two

A vague sense of unease gnawed at Channah. It was not like John Simon to linger in the city. She scanned the horizon in every direction, straining to catch sight of her husband. Seeing only her adopted daughter Miriam and placidly grazing sheep, she decided not to delay gathering the herd to their evening shelter. John Simon would know where to find them when he returned.

She hoped her husband had not run into one of the gangs reported to be going about in Jerusalem beating followers of the Way. The conquerors seemed to close their eyes to these incidents. John Simon told her the Romans did not care what the high priest and the council of the Sanhedrin did so long as taxes were paid and the emperor's authority was not challenged.

"Shall we take the sheep home now?" Channah asked her great uncle Avram.

"Yes." He leaned heavily on his staff as he rose from sitting on a low rock. He stood still for a long moment. "I am worried about him, also."

Channah was not surprised her uncle sensed her unspoken concern. "Perhaps he visited overlong with the disciples and lost track of time." She wanted to believe what she said, but the knot in her stomach refused to loosen.

The pair gathered the supplies they brought with them to the pasture--olive oil, a wineskin, and drinking cups. Miriam joined them as they strolled in the direction of the cave near where their tent stood. Naturally, the herd followed the shepherds wherever they went.

"It is getting late," Miriam commented.

Channah knew her adopted daughter did not refer to the time of leading the sheep to their pen. "Your abba will be home soon."

There was no further conversation as they herded the sheep through a gap in the low stone fence surrounding their dwelling. Once the animals were inside the enclosure, Avram moved a boulder into place to close the opening. Channah and Miriam began to prepare the evening meal.

Avram took one last sweeping look around before accepting a bowl of lentils from Channah. "We must pray for John Simon's safety."

As darkness fell, the sheep settled into their customary spots. Some slept in the open air, while others nestled together inside the small cave that opened into the paddock. Once Channah made sure Miriam was asleep, she took her work bag and slipped out of the dwelling tent. She found her uncle sitting with his back to the boulder gate, sharpening his knife with a whetstone.

Channah sat near Avram. She kept her hands busy, silently carding wool in the pale moonlight.

After some time passed, Avram said, "These are perilous times. I should have gone with him." He inspected the edge of his knife and then polished it more.

"We only want to live quietly and worship in peace," Channah remarked. "Is that so much to ask?"

"It would appear so. Men cry 'peace, peace' but there is no peace." Before long, the old shepherd began to doze, still sitting upright, with his head leaned against the hard rocks of the sheep pen's stone fence.

Channah set her work aside. She knew staying awake was not going to help John Simon, but she could not rest knowing he might be in trouble. Remembering that her uncle said God inhabits the praise of his people, she composed a psalm in her head.

Chapter Three

Channah jumped with fright when the donkey's bray echoed into the night air. A few sheep bleated in protest, and began to mill around. Avram leapt to his feet, just as John Simon vaulted over the stone fence.

She and her uncle spoke simultaneously.

"You are home."

"Thank God."

"Yes." John Simon caressed Channah. "Praise God, I am home at last."

Avram clapped the younger man's shoulder. "We have been worried."

Channah nodded. "What happened?"

"I have much to tell you," John Simon replied. "But first, what is there to eat? I am famished."

Channah hurried to stoke the cooking fire, while her uncle and husband followed at a more leisurely pace.

"I was detained by Roman soldiers," John Simon said. "They took the money we meant for the widows and orphans, but by God's grace I was released." He caught up with Channah and stayed her hands. "There is no need to make fresh bread. Whatever we have will be fine as it is."

John Simon ate a fist-sized loaf of bread in two bites. He dipped a second loaf into his bowl of cold lentil soup.

"What did the soldiers want?" Avram asked.

"I was on my way to the apostle Peter's home to deliver our offering. I turned a corner and blundered into a crowd of people yelling and throwing stones at a house. I have no idea who lives there or what the troublemakers were so angry about." He dipped his bread into the lentils and swallowed another bite. "I turned around, thinking to leave the fracas, but just that quickly soldiers had the way blocked from behind and I was trapped. They took everyone who was in the street to the barracks."

Channah and Avram sat listening as John Simon told them of his narrow escape.

"Thank God the Roman owed a kindness to your father," Avram said. "You will do well not to return to Jerusalem now that your name is known in the barracks."

"There is more." John Simon wiped his bowl clean with the last of his bread. "I walked into the city with another follower of the Way. He told me the disciple James has been beheaded."

"But why?" Channah questioned.

"For being recognized as a leader among the people of the Way. The Sanhedrin means to put a stop to claims that Jesus is the Messiah."

Avram sighed. "At last, the Pharisees and Sadducees can agree on something."

"My traveling companion told me life for followers of the Way is severe in Jerusalem these days. There is a ferocious Pharisee leading the persecution. He is like a mad wolf, ceaselessly searching out believers and having them put in prison. Or worse."

"I heard talk of this man when we took our fleece to the market. Saul is his name." Avram took one of the remaining chunks of bread and broke it into pieces. "He is reputed to be quite a scholar. If that is true, then he, of all people, should know how Jesus fulfilled hundreds of prophesies made down through thousands of years in the holy scriptures. It seems that evidence alone would convince this man, even if he chooses to ignore the miracles the Christ performed."

"This persecution is all about politics and power." John Simon replied. "It has nothing to do with truth."

Channah raised her practical concern. "Do you think we are in danger?"

The men's long silence was an answer of sorts.

At last John Simon spoke. "Yes, Channah."

"Is there anything we can do?" Again, she sensed a reluctance to respond.

"I understand some believers have left Jerusalem," Avram said at last.

It was as if this statement hung in the air, waiting for someone to grasp and examine it.

Finally, John Simon said, "I have heard the same."

Channah felt a sliver of fear slide down her spine. The persecution must be dreadful for people to choose the hardships of exile. "Where did they go?"

"Most went to Alexandria, others to Greece. A few as far as Rome." John Simon shrugged. "Anywhere outside of Israel."

"I expect oppression from the Roman conquerors." Avram's eyes were fixed on the bread in his hands. "But the Sanhedrin making war on our own people? I never thought I would see the day." He consumed the bread and began to scratch in the dirt with the tip of his knife. "Suppose a man wanted to leave our homeland. Where would he go? What would he do?"

Channah suspected her uncle's question was more than idle speculation. Realizing she had no answer, she waited to see if her husband did.

John Simon locked his arms around his bent knees and gazed at the moon. "I suppose it depends. A shepherd would be wise to go to sheep country, some place where he could find employment." After a while, he added, "North, perhaps. Somewhere with good pastureland."

"How?" Avram asked.

John Simon did not move his eyes from the sky. "The port city of Joppa is no more than two-day's distance from here. Ships come through there regularly, bound for a variety of destinations. Alternatively, there are roads all the way to Macedonia and beyond," John Simon continued. "Sea travel is expensive. Then again, overland is harsh."

Avram nodded. "We must think on this."

Channah could hold her tongue no longer. "Uncle, do you mean to say you are considering such a journey?"

"I have long been in prayer on this matter. What are your thoughts, John Simon?"

"I hoped Stephen's stoning was a random incident, because it was mob violence. This man Saul is something else entirely. He is relentless, the kind of zealot who will not rest until he has hunted down all the followers of Jesus."

"Miriam and I will care for the herd if persecution spreads out this far," Channah said. "The two of you can hide until the danger is past. You know of caves they would never find."

John Simon put an arm around her shoulder and leaned toward her until their heads touched. "In Emmaus, Saul and his men took all of the believers prisoner. Women as well as men. Even their children were dragged away in chains."

Channah had prayed to remain steadfast in the face of persecution. However, the thought of someone hurting little Miriam made her shudder.

"I have heard such reports, also. I did not want to alarm you by mentioning them because I hoped the trouble would die down." Avram sheathed his knife. "The sheep are sheared, and the fleece sold. Perhaps it would be a good idea to take the herd to our summer camp high in the mountains early this year."

Chapter Four

Several days later, John Simon and Channah led their herd to a wide meadow where shepherds often congregated to feed their flocks together. Channah enjoyed going to community pastures to visit with other shepherd families. It gave her the rare opportunity to sit and talk with the other women when not tending to the animals. Miriam made friends easily among the girls. Avram loved spinning yarns with the other old men. John Simon was less social, normally preferring to spend his time alone among his sheep or with his family. On this occasion, however, Channah noticed he engaged the other shepherds in frequent conversations.

After a community meal the first evening, Channah and the other women gathered around the cooking fire to socialize. She and Miriam sat quietly carding wool, listening more than talking.

"My husband is concerned about what is happening in Jerusalem," a woman commented. "He said they are arresting those who follow the Way."

"Yes," a woman Channah knew by the name Mary said. "We heard one of their top men was beheaded. James, I believe is the name. My cousin said he was a close friend of the prophet from Nazareth, the one the Romans crucified."

"Well, that should have put the whole bunch to flight," a tall, spare woman commented. "We Jews have worshipped the same way for thousands of years. Why let a few agitators change our religion now? They are going to bring the Romans down hard on all of us if we are not careful."

"The followers of Jesus only want peace as they seek to live quiet lives that please God," Channah said.

The tall woman whirled toward her. “Those people of the Way are nothing but troublemakers.” With narrowed eyes, she demanded, “Are you one of them?”

“Come, now.” Mary stood before Channah could answer. “What shall we prepare for the community meal tomorrow evening? We must decide what each of us is to contribute.”

Channah noticed the tall woman staring at her several times. She was relieved when the group began to melt away.

“We must withdraw from this area,” Avram said quietly as soon as his family gathered away from the others. “There is a man among us with a fire in his belly against the Way. I feel strongly this is not a safe place.”

John Simon glanced left and right. “What are your thoughts, Channah?”

“I felt strangely uncomfortable among the women this evening. There was one who was openly hostile toward followers of the Way. When shall we go?” she questioned, drawing Miriam closer to her side.

“Tonight, while most of the camp sleeps is the best time for us to depart.” John Simon examined smooth stones within his reach. Now and then he tucked one into a leather pouch. “Those performing the night watch know only our own sheep will separate themselves and go with us when they hear us call for them.”

Accustomed to traveling to far pastures, each member of the household knew the preparation routine. Channah, who was the most skillful with the donkey, coaxed the animal into her harness and hitched up the cart. Meanwhile, the men loaded the cart with bedding, tools, and food. Little Miriam was responsible for gathering and loading the cooking and eating utensils.

By the time the waning moon joined lesser lights in the night sky, the family was ready to move on. With a nod of his head, John Simon led the way. Channah followed, using handfuls of grain to encourage the donkey forward. As soon as they were near the broad flat space where the sheep were sleeping, John Simon went and spoke to the men standing watch. At his signal, Channah called out to her herd. Miriam tapped on a little drum, and their animals awoke, bleated, and came forward.

Channah and the donkey cart led the herd toward home. Meanwhile, John Simon and Avram walked behind the sheep to keep the stragglers moving. After a while, John Simon caught up with Channah and lifted the yawning Miriam into the cart. Channah shifted pots and cups aside to tuck her daughter into a temporary bed. The girl fell asleep almost immediately.

Instead of falling back, John Simon took Channah's hand and walked beside her. "Our homeland has become more dangerous every day. For some time, I have thought we should relocate." They walked a few steps in silence before he added, "I have hesitated because of Avram. We cannot leave him behind, but I wonder if he is able to travel or adjust to foreign ways. Now that whole families are being killed, my first concern is to protect you and Miriam."

"Uncle is not as strong as he used to be, but for a man of his age he is vigorous." Despite the seriousness of the matter, Channah smiled. She once entertained doubts about marrying John Simon, but was now so grateful he was her husband. Not only had he shown her depths of love she never expected, he had accepted her adopted daughter as his own child.

He leaned and kissed her cheek. "We must pray about this matter." He released her hand, slowed his pace, and disappeared into the night.

Channah walked on, refusing to let herself dwell on the softness of her fleece bedding. Her thoughts were more for the next day than for the distant future. She planned to feed the sheep from her stores of grain rather than taking them out to pasture after they arrived home. Everyone, including the animals, needed to rest. After a few hours of sleep, perhaps she could begin to consider the preparations involved in leaving Israel. At the moment, thoughts of such an undertaking overwhelmed her.

Chapter Five

"Someone moved the gate stone," Channah said as her husband caught up with her. They were always careful to replace the big rock that closed the gap in the stone fence when they left their home base.

"Wait here." John Simon made his way through the open gate among the sheep already streaming into their familiar paddock.

"The gate was left open," Channah said when her uncle came to stand beside her.

"Are you certain? I remember seeing John Simon roll the stone into place when we left for the community pasture," After a moment, he added, "Someone is here. Or has been."

Channah's hand flew to her throat "Our tent." The sides of their dwelling had cuts running from near the top all the way to the ground.

Avram patted her shoulder and went inside the fence. He reached the cave entrance next to their tent just as John Simon emerged from the cave. "We have had visitors," John Simon declared. "They seem to be gone now."

As quickly as she could, Channah unhitched the donkey. She staked the animal where she could graze and lie down. Then, leaving Miriam asleep in the cart, she hurried to her tent. It was a mess. All of the crocks were shattered, their contents strewn on the ground. Her storage shelf had been pulled down and broken. She sensed something was missing. Yes, where she kept high stacks of sheepskins and fleece, there was now only an empty space. Out of habit, she exited the tent through the entry flap, although she could easily have walked through one of the many vertical slashes.

She snuggled against John Simon, hoping to draw on his strength. “It will take me a week to mend our tent. Was it a bear?”

“No.” John Simon pulled her closer and rested his chin on her head. “All of this destruction was wrought by human hands.”

Channah felt tears forming. “The thieves smashed our crocks. There are beans and lentils and date cakes scattered everywhere. They took our fleece and skins, too.”

“No,” Avram said. “Instead of taking the skins and fleece, they burned them in the large water trough. The intruders came to destroy, not to steal.”

“But why?” Channah asked.

“Because we are followers of Jesus,” John Simon answered through clenched teeth.

She pulled away from her husband enough to look up into his face. “How do you know this?”

“They left a message on the wall in the cave,” Avram growled.

Channah took a step toward the cave. John Simon held her arm. “It is not a good thing to see.”

“I must.” She hurried into the mouth of the cave. There on the wall, someone had scratched crude figures, two men, a woman, and a child, all crucified. *They know who and how many we are.* John Simon was right. She wished she had not seen the drawings.

Trembling with fear, Channah walked back to the paddock where John Simon and Avram stood. Before any of them could speak, their neighbor, the shepherd Josiah stumbled inside their fence and fell at their feet.

“Thank God I am in time,” Josiah said in between heavy panting. “Water.”

Moving toward her tent as quickly as possible without alarming the sheep, Channah remembered she had no dishes left there. She turned back and brought a cup and a wineskin from the cart that still stood just outside the paddock fence. She held the cup while John Simon poured it full of wine.

Avram knelt, raised Josiah's upper body, and supported him while he drank.

Without being asked, Channah returned to the cart to fetch three date cakes and a stale loaf of bread. She was glad to find her daughter was still asleep. She quickly adjusted Miriam's blanket before taking the food to Josiah.

"I came to warn you," Josiah said as soon as he was able to speak. "That cursed Saul of Tarsus has whipped the people of Bethlehem into a murderous frenzy. They are arresting all of the Jesus followers in this area. Someone betrayed us and turned our names over to the high priest."

"But our synagogue leader has proclaimed Jesus is the Messiah," Avram protested.

"He was the first victim. The mob stoned him to death."

Avram guided John Simon's arms to take over Josiah's support. "There is something I must do." He rose and strode away, unsheathing his knife as he went.

"I must be on my way," Josiah said. "I have to warn the other shepherds." He attempted to stand, but stumbled and fell back.

"You do not have the strength to run to the next camp," John Simon said. "Rest here while I will bring you the horse I keep hidden away." He stood and ran from the paddock. Frightened sheep bleated and skittered away, but he did not seem to notice.

Channah poured more wine and offered it to Josiah. He sat up and drank. Then he attacked the date cakes and bread she gave him.

"Did he say *horse*?" Josiah asked between bites. "No hill country shepherd has a horse. What is your husband talking about?"

"John Simon has a horse," Channah assured him. "A fine Arabian stallion. You can cover ground in no time on his back. Let me know if you want something else to eat." In the moments since Avram and John Simon departed, she realized they could not remain in their home camp with evil doers rampaging through the hills.

She harnessed her donkey to the cart and offered her a handful of grain. "Forgive me." She stroked the donkey's face. "I know you are tired, old friend. So am I, but this cannot be helped."

Soon John Simon returned. He dismounted and tethered his horse near the outside of the fence.

"Ride him as you would a donkey," John Simon said. "But be aware he has much more speed. If you fall off, he will not run away. He has been trained to wait for you." He squatted beside Josiah. "When you have warned the other shepherds, turn the horse loose. He can survive in the wild. Bury the saddle and reins. You do not want the Romans to find you with a war horse or their military equipment."

"But how—" Josiah began.

John Simon waved a hand. "It is best not to know. You cannot reveal what you have not been told."

"You need have no concern that I will be captured." Josiah ducked his head. "As soon as I spread the word, I will kill myself."

Channah gasped.

John Simon put an arm around Josiah. "No. As followers of the Way, we cannot take a God-given life, not even our own. Tell me, why would consider such a dreadful thing?"

"The marauders took my wife and children prisoner before I came home."

"I am sorry," John Simon said. "Perhaps you can rescue them. No matter what happens, you must not commit suicide."

Channah glanced aside to see her uncle placing a small object into the cart. *He must have dug up the little wooden chest where he keeps his storehouse of coins.*

Avram joined the group. "We must go."

"Yes," Josiah agreed. "Run for your lives and God be with you." He stood and the four of them walked through the gate. "Meanwhile, I must warn the others."

John Simon helped Josiah onto the horse's back. He untied the reins and placed them in Josiah's hands. "We can take only a small flock with us. The rest of the herd is yours now. Sell the sheep and take the money to the Roman barracks in Jerusalem. The centurion there takes bribes. If you pay him enough, perhaps he will arrange for your wife and children to be released."

"But if I sell your animals, what will you do when you return?"

"We will not be back," John Simon assured him.

"Have no more thoughts of destroying yourself." Avram patted Josiah's thigh. "There is always hope in the Lord."

"I must confess to you what I did. I was desperate to get away from Bethlehem and back to my family." Josiah turned sorrowful eyes toward them. "To escape from the mob, I denied my faith." Tears streamed down his cheeks.

The stallion took a leap and began to gallop away, with Josiah crouched low over his back.

Chapter Six

◆ With Miriam's help, Channah loaded what additional food she could salvage into the cart. Meanwhile, John Simon cleaned and filled the watering troughs. Avram opened up the stored grain, providing food that would sustain the herd for many days.

With the quick preparations completed, Channah led Miriam and the donkey cart away from the home she loved. Her husband and uncle joined her with a flock of a dozen sheep trailing after them.

"Where are we going?" Miriam asked.

Channah had the same question. She would have offered a suggestion if she had one, but Jerusalem was the only place she had ever been outside these hills. She knew her uncle had traveled to various places, but always within Israel. She hoped her husband had some idea of a suitable destination. At the moment, the need for sleep crowded other thoughts from her mind.

John Simon said, "We can pick up the road to the coast by cutting to the northwest and bypassing Jerusalem. Joppa is the nearest port."

"Good." Avram's words came slowly. "I have seen boats, but I have never been on one."

"A ship can take us where we want to go much easier and faster than traveling overland."

"We must let our sheep rest soon." Channah ended her sentence with a big yawn.

John Simon rested an arm around her shoulders. "Perhaps you and Miriam should ride in the cart for a while."

"No." Channah smiled at her husband's thoughtful offer. "It is hard enough for the donkey to pull our belongings without sleeping. We need not add to her burden." She saw the disappointment in her daughter's upturned face and reached to pat her dark head. "We will rest when we stop for the sheep to graze."

They traveled in silence for what seemed to Channah to be a very long time. She was relieved when John Simon said, "This meadow with a stream running through it looks like a good place for a brief stop."

By dawn, the milking was done, the family fed, and the morning prayers said. Channah put the leftover sheep's milk into a tanned skin and tied it to the cart. She had attempted to sleep, but to no avail. Although no one spoke of fear, there was noticeable tension in the air. She tried not to be obvious about listening for any sound that indicated they were being pursued. Even the animals were unusually jumpy.

John Simon placed his drinking cup on the cart and shook out his tunic. "After we are past Jerusalem, we can take a more leisurely pace. We should reach Joppa tomorrow or the next day."

"And where will we go from there?" Channah asked.

"There are numerous choices. For the next several months, the weather will be good for sailing. Ships from all over the world put into the port at Joppa." John Simon rubbed his chin. "They are bound for cities stretching from Rome all the way south to Egypt. Do you have a preference?"

Although she appreciated being consulted, Channah had nothing to contribute. Neither, she suspected, did her uncle. "You must make the choice, Husband. Uncle Avram and I have no knowledge of the outside world." The enormity of what they were doing struck her with a mental blow that left her breathless.

"I am thinking of Ephesus, if we have enough money for our passage there." John Simon answered. "The city has a sizeable Jewish community. My Greek is good, and Avram knows enough commercial Greek to communicate passably. We should be able to find work in the pastures around there until our little flock grows large enough to support us."

"I am glad you know these things. If Ephesus is the destination you think best, then of course we should go there." Channah again marveled that she had initially resisted marrying John Simon. Since then, she had learned to love him for his quiet strength and steadfast faith. What would she do without him to rely on now? Her husband seldom mentioned his past, but Channah knew he had spent his early years in Ephesus. "Do you have family in Asia?" she dared to ask.

"I am related to people there." He began to tighten the donkey's harness. "But they will not help us."

The donkey made it clear she did not wish to leave the patch of grass she munched on. "This animal is so stubborn," Miriam complained.

"No, she is merely tired." Channah rubbed the donkey's ears, not knowing how either one of them could resume their efforts. "Come now, old friend," she whispered. "Somewhere beyond Jerusalem, you will have a good rest and plenty of grain."

John Simon led the way toward the distant walls of Jerusalem. After a while they turned to parallel the walls, and finally angled away from them, headed in a direction Channah supposed must lead to the coastline of the great sea.

Channah gave Miriam the last of the bread loaves to eat as they trudged forward on a packed, worn pathway. "I will bake more bread when we stop to rest," she assured her daughter. Then she remembered she had not set any dough to rise. Although her family preferred the lightness of yeasty loaves, they would have to make do with unleavened bread today.

John Simon veered from the pathway occasionally, only to return and march on. At last, he returned from one of his forays with good news. “There is a good resting place with grass and water.” He pointed. “Behind those rocks.”

Channah grasped the donkey’s halter and led her from the road. She wondered which of them was more grateful for a respite. Patches of grass were flattened. “We are not the first to pasture here,” she observed to no one in particular.

“There must be a fair amount of traffic on this back road. Otherwise, it would get overgrown and disappear, since there are no paving stones.” John Simon unloaded a cooking pot from the cart.

“Will we stay here long enough for my bread to rise?” Channah asked, hoping for an affirmative answer. The bread was a side issue to her weariness. She dreaded having to walk on again.

“It would be good to rest here until tomorrow morning.” John Simon wiped his brow. “The animals need sleep, and so do we.”

“Yes,” Avram, standing nearby, agreed. “I must admit this old man is exhausted.” He tapped his staff on the ground lightly. “Is anyone pursuing us?”

“I doubt it,” John Simon replied. “From the top of the rocks, I saw only one small group behind us. They were some distance away and had the appearance of a family.”

Channah took Miriam’s hand in hers. “Let us prepare our meal.”

The family had hardly finished eating when Miriam laid her head in Channah’s lap and fell asleep. John Simon stood and took up his staff. “I will keep watch first,” he announced, as if there was any doubt.

Avram nodded his agreement and collapsed onto the fleece bedding laid out on the ground near the donkey cart.

Channah quickly put away her cooking utensils. Although she had only packed for a short stay in the pasture, she had the bare essentials. She chased thoughts of her shattered crocks from her mind and went to sit by John Simon on a rocky elevation.

He smiled and put an arm around her shoulder. “You should be sleeping.”

“I am too tired to go to sleep, if that makes any sense.”

“It does.”

They sat in silence, watching their tiny flock. Taking advantage of being alone with her husband, Channah felt free to speak of the thoughts that nagged at her. “What will we do when we get to Joppa?”

John Simon shrugged his shoulders. “Sell the cart and the donkey. Hope we have enough to pay for our passage on a big ship headed north. If not, we must sell the sheep as well. Worst case, we will walk. The Via Maritima follows the coast and would be easier than climbing over the mountains. Somehow, we will make our way to Ephesus or some other place where we will be safe.”

She found comfort in her husband’s words. His plan lacked detail, but his confidence was contagious. “And then?”

“We will trust God to provide and go on living as best we can until he gathers us to himself.”

She snuggled closer to him. “Do you think it is wrong to take Miriam away with us? What if her father has a change of heart and wants to reclaim her. He would not know where to search.”

“We have to take her with us, either that or turn her over to the caretakers of the widows and orphans at the church in Jerusalem. Miriam’s father deserted her and the rest of his family years ago, Channah. Why would he try to find her now? We will take good care of her.”

Channah chewed her bottom lip. “She has the best possible father in you.”

“And a wonderful mother.”

“I wish—” Channah stopped herself, not wanting to remind herself or her husband of her barrenness. Thinking of the crude drawing the vandals left at their home, she asked, “Do the Romans really crucify children?”

“They have been known to, in rare circumstances.” He peered into her eyes. “Why do you ask?”

“That drawing in the cave,” Channah replied. “You were right. I should never have looked in there. Those gruesome pictures haunt me, especially the one of a child.”

“Only the Romans have the authority to crucify. Those drawings were done by Pharisees, or Sadducees, or some of their misguided followers to frighten us.”

“And they smashed all of our crocks.” Channah did not understand why this smallest of losses made her start crying. Once she started, the emotions of the past two days engulfed her.

“This is hard for you, I know.” John Simon held her close while the tears flowed.

“I do not want Miriam or Uncle Avram to see me cry,” she confessed when she was able to speak again.

“You are entitled to a few tears. They know, as I do, how strong you are.” He kissed the top of her head. “Now go and get some rest. Tomorrow will be a long day.”

Chapter Seven

Joppa was a beautiful city, situated on a rocky shelf overlooking the deep blue waters of the Mediterranean, which the Romans called their sea. John Simon told Channah that Joppa was famous for its gardens and fruit trees. Despite its beauty, the city had a stench that made her stomach turn. "What is that horrible smell?" she asked as they approached the coastline.

"All port cities have a distinctive aroma," John Simon said. "It comes from rotting fish and garbage cast into the water."

Channah wrinkled her nose. "I find it most unpleasant."

"I have good news for you, then." He smiled. "Avram spoke with someone who told him of a place outside the city, away from the water, where people of the Way gather to wait for ships or caravans. We can camp there until I am able to make arrangements for our passage.

The campground was, as John Simon reported, far enough from the sea that the water was not visible. Still, Channah could not escape the disgusting odor of the sea water. It seemed to cling to her, making her feel mildly nauseous from time to time.

At the campsite, it was a relief to be among other followers of Jesus, where Channah felt her family was safer than they would be alone in a big city. The evening meal was a community effort, with Channah contributing a large quantity of dried beans and quite a few small loaves of bread. Sitting with the other women, she felt comfortable, though not quite at home.

"Where are you going?" the well-dressed woman next to her asked.

"Ephesus is our hope," Channah replied. "And you?"

"Alexandria, in Egypt. My husband has a cousin there."

They exchanged small talk about their families and places of origin. Suddenly, the woman lowered her voice and leaned near Channah's ear. "See the family over there? The bunch with the strange hair? They should not allow those people to stay here."

Although Channah was not clear who 'they' were, it was easy to spot the family the woman meant. A man and woman with hair the color of dried flax sat apart with three young children. "Why not?" she asked.

"Well," the woman answered, with lifted eyebrows. "The man is employed by the Roman government, or was until a few days ago. Somehow he ran afoul of that rabid dog from Tarsus, who in case you have not heard is a Roman citizen on top of everything else. Saul managed to have this man discharged from his job." She leaned even closer, almost touching Channah's ear. "I have heard the husband is a God-fearer."

"What does that mean?"

The woman did a double take. "They are *gentiles,* my dear. That man has probably not been circumcised."

"But if they are being persecuted as followers of Jesus—"

The woman interrupted her. "We would *never* have shared a meal with such people in Jerusalem. They are unclean."

"Oh," was the only response Channah could manage. She was aware that shepherds were considered a cut below people who earned their livelihood in some other way. However, the division between her and her companion went beyond social status. John Simon's appearance did not give away his half-Roman blood, although he made no secret of his parentage back home in the hill country. She ate in silence, pondering a secret that only she and her husband knew—that he had never been circumcised.

Channah excused herself as soon as she felt she could without seeming to be impolite. Then she called Miriam away from the other little girls and retreated to the small plot of earth her family temporarily occupied. John Simon and Avram had erected the small travel tent they used for pasturing at home. It was barely large enough to hold their unrolled bedding, but provided an adequate shelter. After some discussion, they decided the sheep should pass the night in the tent.

John Simon took two fleece bed rolls and set them on the ground. “If we sleep here in front of the tent flap, there will be no need to set a night watch over the animals.”

After sunset, Channah snuggled close to John Simon, enjoying the warmth of his nearness. She pondered that day’s conversation with the woman who objected to a gentile family in the camp, suspecting the woman would consider her husband to be unclean if she knew of his heritage. However, as she typically did, Channah kept her thoughts to herself.

The next morning, while John Simon and Avram went to the port to inquire about their passage to Ephesus, Channah and Miriam took their little flock of a dozen sheep to a nearby well. The pale-haired woman was there also, drawing water. She glanced their direction, smiled, and spoke a cheerful, “Shalom.”

Channah responded with the same greeting, adding. “I am Channah. My daughter’s name is Miriam. I have seen your family at the campsite.”

"Yes, we are so grateful to have a place to stay until our caravan leaves Joppa. I am Lora."

Channah was intrigued by Lora's appearance. Her sky-colored eyes were even more exotic than her hair.

Lora drew a bucket from the well and slowly poured water into a carrying pouch. "I have not seen you before. Are you newly arrived?"

"We came to the encampment yesterday afternoon," Channah answered. She drew water and added it to the stationary trough where her sheep stood drinking. She nudged two fat ewes apart to make room for a yearling. "Keep an eye on the sheep and make sure all of them get a chance at the water," she instructed Miriam.

"Will you be joining the caravan?" Lora asked.

Channah drew more water for her sheep. "No, we are planning to travel by sea. My husband and uncle went to the port this morning to see what we should do. I have never been on a ship before. Have you?"

"We came from Rome by sea. It is a much faster and safer way to travel." She hoisted the strap of her water bag over her shoulder. "We would go that way if we could. However, the man named Saul managed to have everything we owned confiscated. So, we have no means to pay for a ship to take us north."

If she knew Lora better, Channah would have embraced her. As it was, she merely said, "I am so sorry."

Lora patted the top of Miriam's head as she passed her. "We are honored to suffer for the name of Jesus. And to think, we were not even born Jewish." She smiled. "My family and I are greatly blessed."

Channah watched Lora walk down the pathway to the campsite, with her golden hair shimmering in the early morning sunlight. She admired the gentile woman's outlook. She had not considered being chased away from her home as something to be thankful for. It was an idea she felt a need to think about.

Chapter Eight

Toward evening, the men returned to the camp bursting with news. “A ship came into port this afternoon with an itinerary that includes Ephesus,” John Simon announced. “And we have more than enough coinage to cover our passage.

John Simon put a hand on each of Channah’s shoulders and looked into her face. “The ship departs early tomorrow morning, but their deck is crowded with so much cargo there is barely room for our family. We cannot take our sheep or the donkey on board. Can we be ready?”

“Yes. I will pack our few possessions into a compact bundle inside the folded-up tent.” The short preparation time did not trouble Channah. She was accustomed to moving among campsites. However, she did find the thought of parting with the last of their animals painful.

“There is a man coming to look at the flock before sundown.” Avram knelt and patted a sheep’s rump. “I have no doubt he will find them satisfactory and will make us a reasonable price.”

“That leaves only the donkey and cart to dispose of.” John Simon rubbed his chin. “They would be a great help getting us to the ship, but once there what would we do with them?”

Avram looked up from his kneeling position. “I observed a man arrive at the port with his cart today. He sold it to a dockside merchant.”

“He did,” John Simon agreed. “But he received a paltry price, nothing near what his cart and animal were worth. The merchants at the port know people about to sail away have no time to bargain or find another buyer.”

Channah was struck by an idea. "Suppose someone here in the camp plans to travel by land. They could take us to our ship and then keep our donkey and cart."

John Simon smiled at her. "Do you have anyone in mind?"

As she often did, Channah marveled at how well her husband knew her. "I was thinking of the people with the pale skin and hair, the family that stays to themselves on the far fringes of the camp. I met Lora, the wife, at the well. She told me everything they had was confiscated in Jerusalem."

"Why?" Avram asked. "They are not Jews."

"No," Channah agreed. "But they are former God-fearers who now follow the Way. Her husband somehow got into an argument with that Saul of Tarsus fellow. Lora said they are joining a northbound caravan because they cannot afford passage on a ship."

John Simon hitched his belt. "I will go and speak with the blond man. An overland journey is difficult. His small children can ride in the cart to keep pace with the caravan."

After her husband walked away, Channah turned to question Avram. "The gentile man is blind?"

"No," Avram answered with a grin. "He said blond, not blind. It is another way to describe yellow hair." He nodded toward John Simon's retreating back. "It is good to help our neighbors, most especially those who are suffering for the name of Jesus." The old man sat staring into the distance for a moment before speaking again. "You have given me an idea, Channah. Instead of selling our sheep, perhaps John Simon can find someone who will care for them and continue to share milk in the camp after we leave."

"Will my lamb have to stay behind, too?" Miriam asked.

"Yes, child." Avram drew the girl close to his side. "But we will have another flock in Ephesus, and you may take your choice of the firstborn lambs."

"It will not be the same," Miriam protested.

"Nothing will ever be quite the same for us again." Avram spoke as if to himself. "Nevertheless, all will be well. No matter where we go, we will have our faith and we will be together."

Miriam smiled. "And next Spring I shall have a spotted lamb."

Channah reached to place her hands on the shoulders of her daughter and her kneeling uncle, as if to absorb their optimism.

Well before dawn, John Simon removed their tent pegs from the ground. He and Avram spread the collapsed structure on the ground. Channah placed the pegs, her dough trough, cooking utensils, and her wool-working tools on the tent and folded it shut. Each member of the family rolled up their bedding with their one extra set of clothing and nonperishable food for the journey inside. Miriam passed out loaves of bread while the adults silently loaded the donkey cart.

Channa noticed the gentile man waiting silently by the cart, holding the donkey's reins. The cap pulled low over his ears hid his startling hair. She took a step in his direction and rubbed the donkey's ears. "She is a good animal, but she is more easily persuaded than forced. A handful of grain is all you will need to convince her to move forward, even when the load is heavy."

The man nodded his understanding. "Thank you."

Channah ran a hand over the donkey's neck. "Goodbye, old friend," she whispered, hoping the gentile did not think her peculiar for engaging in conversation with a donkey. Her stomach churned with the difficulty of parting with her animals. Her life had been dominated by caring for them every day. Now she could only hope their new owners would treat them well.

Soon the passage was paid and the bundles were loaded onto the ship. The stench of the sea water was so strong it made Channah nauseous. She felt slightly better after losing her breakfast.

"Will the movement be smoother as soon as we put out to sea?" she asked.

"Perhaps we will have calm waters," John Simon said without conviction. He put an arm over her shoulder. "Things will settle down once you get your sea legs."

"I have never seen anything like this," Avram commented. "Even on the Sea of Galilee, the shore is always visible in the distance. He pointed away from Joppa. "Out there, I see only water."

John Simon turned and leaned on the ship's railing. "The small ships follow the shoreline and stop at every town and village along the way. This vessel is making straight to Cyprus. Once there, we should be able to find another ship going to Ephesus. We are likely to be there before the end of the month."

Miriam opened the bag containing leftover bread and offered it to Channah. "Would you like a loaf?"

"No." She held up a hand to maintain a safe distance between herself and the food. "No, thank you." She never expected to be hungry again.

Soon after the ship left the port, Channah did something unusual. She unrolled and stretched out on her fleece bedding, pulled the blanket over her head, and went to sleep. She roused occasionally to take note of Miriam sitting beside her, quietly carding wool. Earlier, she planned to take out her dough trough and set bread to rise. Now, nothing seemed urgent enough to crawl from beneath her covers.

John Simon brought her broth, but Channah refused it. She turned away and moaned, hoping her inevitable death would come quickly. After a fitful nap, she roused long enough to throw up into a crock someone had thoughtfully left within reach.

Channah became aware that John Simon was shaking her shoulder. “Wake up. We are coming into Caesarea. How do you feel?”

“Not good.” She opened her eyes. “I thought we were going to Cyprus.”

“That is this ship’s usual route. But the captain is making an unplanned stop overnight.” He smoothed back her hair. “We can get off and spend some time on land. It will help settle your stomach.”

Channah lifted herself on an elbow. “I will try.”

“Avram has agreed to stay on board and guard our possessions. Miriam will keep him company.” John Simon helped her to her feet. She walked leaning heavily against her husband, feeling dizzy and nauseous.

“Miriam is not ill?”

“No. Only you have the sickness of the sea.” He helped her from the gangplank onto the dock. “And normally, you are the heartiest one of us.”

John Simon guided Channah to a shoreside stand where small, golden-brown roots were on display.

The toothless vendor stirred a pot of clear broth. He nodded toward Channah. “You have the look of one who did not enjoy crossing the waves.” He dipped a cup into the broth, held it high, and slowly dribbled the liquid back into the pot. “In these roots, you will find the cure.”

Despite Channah's weak protest, John Simon paid a high price for a portion of the vendor's broth. "Here, drink this." He handed her the cup. "The sailors assured me it will help you feel better."

She took a sip, wrinkled her nose, and forced herself to drink. Sure enough, whether it was the soup or merely having her feet fixed on solid ground, Channah's nausea gradually subsided.

At dusk, John Simon returned to the ship, leaving Channah waiting for him at the gangplank. He came back with a blanket and smiled in his distinctive, lopsided way. "As long as we stay nearby, we can remain on the shore tonight. The captain told me the prisoner will be delivered tomorrow morning."

Sleeping under the stars in their clothing was nothing new to either of them. However, the stone-like composition of the jetty was noticeably harder than the grassy earth of a pasture. "Concrete," John Simon remarked, patting the surface. "The Romans built these docks from it. They use it for everything."

As everything became quiet, Channah was pleasantly surprised to find the sound of the lapping sea calming. When she reluctantly agreed to marry John Simon, she doubted her uncle's assurance they would learn to love each other. She thought how wise her uncle was, because her husband endeared himself to her a little more each day.

Chapter Nine

John Simon nudged Channah awake. The tentative promise of dawn highlighted the outline of different-sized vessels in the harbor. “We have to get back on board the ship,” he said, as he folded their blanket.

Channah followed him up the gangplank. The waves that lulled her to sleep the night before now rhythmically rocked the anchored ship. She told herself the gentle motion could not have an immediate effect. Nevertheless, she began to feel slightly queasy.

Avram sat snoring on the ship’s deck, sleeping in his usual upright position. Miriam slept curled up against him with her head resting on his thigh. Channah stepped around them to rummage through her food bag. She took a stale loaf of bread for herself and one for John Simon, along with a generous chunk of cheese to offer him.

She expected her husband to be nearby, but did not immediately see him. Leaving her uncle and daughter asleep, she wandered back toward the gangplank. She found John Simon leaning on the rail. He was turned toward the outline of Caesarea.

Channah stood next to him, silently offering him his breakfast. “Is Ephesus like Caesarea?” she asked.

“In some ways.” He accepted the food and nibbled at the cheese. “You will see a huge pagan temple and a grand marketplace there, but nothing like Herod’s palace.” He gestured toward a fortress-like complex resting on a promontory that jutted out into the water. “I have heard there are beautiful pools around the main building, overlooking the sea. And, of course, a dreadful dungeon down below. If I am not mistaken, that is where John the Baptist was beheaded.”

“Who?” Channah questioned.

"A prophet, one of the first to proclaim Jesus as the Messiah." John Simon ate in silence, continuing to study the awakening coast.

The sound of footsteps on the gangplank distracted Channah. She turned to see a well-dressed, middle-aged man stride onto the deck, closely followed by a Roman soldier.

John Simon leaned near her ear and whispered. "The ship had to make an unscheduled stop to pick up a prisoner, and now I see he is being guarded by a centurion. He must be someone important."

Channah wondered how her husband knew the soldier was a centurion. There must have been something distinctive about his clothing. Ordinarily, she would have asked. However, she feared speaking would disturb the uneasy temporary truce with her stomach.

She rested her back against the railing and watched the sailors begin their preparations for leaving the port. The ship's captain greeted the centurion and nodded to the prisoner. "We will get underway now, if you are ready."

"Yes," the centurion answered. "The sooner the better."

"Did you not observe the high, wispy clouds racing through the sky last evening?" The prisoner spoke with authority. "And this morning, my joints ache. There will be a sea storm today or tomorrow. You would be wise to tarry in the port a while longer."

The centurion laughed. "I am certain the captain has navigated through more than a few storms. Aching joints notwithstanding, let us be on our way."

After the men moved away, John Simon turned his back to the rail and peered at the sky.

Although she had a good night's sleep, Channah felt a crushing weariness. Her nature was not to give in to physical weakness, but the bobbing of the ship defeated her. "I will go and lie down now." Without waiting for John Simon to acknowledge her departure, she walked swiftly to the cramped space assigned to her family.

She found her uncle and daughter awake and munching on stale bread. "Are you sick again, Ima?" Miriam asked.

"Just tired." Channah thought what a foolish thing that was to say first thing in the morning, but she did not have the energy to explain further. She lay on the partially unrolled bedding and fell asleep.

She was startled awake by something crashing against a bulkhead.

"You are awake. Good." John Simon's face told her something was wrong. "Take Miriam and go to the place where we stood by the rail this morning."

As soon as Channah stood, she lurched against a post. "What is happening?"

"A storm," Avram answered. "A bad one."

"Take Miriam and go now." John Simon said. "No ship can hold together in waves such as these."

Between the violent rocking and sailors scurrying in every direction, Channah had a hard time making her way to the railing. Raindrops began to come at her sideways. The wind howled and swirled, pushing people and objects in every direction.

She could not hear Miriam's voice, but the movement of the child's lips said, "I am afraid."

Channah wrapped her arms around her child and held her tightly. As sailors lowered a small boat over the side of the ship, she wondered if she should try to get Miriam into the boat before her husband and uncle arrived. However, before she could move against the wind, members of the crew filled the boat and rowed away.

Avram's head emerged from below the deck. As he backed away from the rope ladder, John Simon appeared. They were carrying two large wooden doors, which they brought to the rail where Channah and Miriam waited.

John Simon shouted something. Channah shook her head and put her hands behind her ears to indicate that she could not hear him. He held up one finger, pointed to himself, and then to the water. Next, he held up two fingers aimed at the doors. Three fingers, then to Channah and Miriam. He made a diving motion over the rail. Surely, he did not want her and their little girl to jump into that angry sea.

A sail came loose, crashing onto the deck. Channah could not hear her own scream. She turned away in time to see her uncle lowering the doors over the side of the ship with heavy ropes. Avram leaned over the rail for a moment, then motioned to Channah to go.

She looked down at the roiling water, mesmerized, unable to think, too frightened to move.

Avram grabbed Miriam and threw her overboard.

Channah saw John Simon, moving like a fish, take hold of their daughter and lift her onto what appeared to be a raft. She felt Avram pick her up. Before she could resist, her uncle tossed her into the sea. She sank into the shockingly cold water, certain she was about to die.

Without understanding why, Channah fought the strong arms that enfolded her. She felt the roughness of wood against her cheek. Then she was next to Miriam, coughing and sputtering. Someone took her hand and tied it to the end of a rope. She wrapped an arm around Miriam as waves tossed them about, often washing forcefully over Channah. She held on with all her strength, assuring Miriam's little arm remained securely tied to a rope.

Channah saw chunks of the ship's hull flying loose, falling into the water around her. She became aware of Avram holding to the side of the makeshift raft, pushing away from the disintegrating ship. "Where is John Simon?" she yelled several times. If there was an answer, she could not hear it.

For what seemed to be a very long time, it was all Channah could do to hold onto Miriam. She lost her grip as a giant wave swept over them and the doors separated from each other. As soon as she could see what happened, Channah lunged toward where her little girl lay. However, she could not escape the rope that held her hand. Frantically, she tried to untie herself, although uncertain what she would do when she was free. She stopped struggling when she realized the two doors had separated and were now too far apart for her to reach. Avram still clung to Miriam's door. Most of his body was submerged. Only his arms and head were visible.

Channah scanned the churning water as best she could to keep track of her uncle and child. Within a short time, they were out of sight.

After a long time, sunlight broke through the clouds. The door still tossed wildly, but the waves ceased to sweep over her. Being careful to keep a tight hold on her rope, Channah sat upright and looked around. There was debris in the water around her, but no other living human being was in sight.

She pushed the wet hair from her face and prayed earnestly. Her plea was not for herself, but for Avram, John Simon, and most especially Miriam to be rescued.

After a while, Channah realized her leg hurt. She noticed her clothing was torn. Blood oozed from a long cut on her right thigh. She had no idea how or when the wound occurred. She covered herself as well as she could with the remnant of her tunic, again imploring God to save her daughter.

Chapter Ten

Avram kicked his legs as vigorously as he could. Hours of being in the water left him weak with hunger and fatigue. "Do you see a ship anywhere?" he asked Miriam.

She shook her head. "Only water. If I stand up, I can see more."

"Scoot closer so I can hold on to you."

Miriam obeyed, sliding sideways until her feet were almost in Avram's face. He grasped her ankles while she struggled to stand on the rocking door. After two unsuccessful attempts, the girl managed to arise. She planted her feet widely apart, but soon fell to a sitting position.

"I saw land over there." Miriam pointed an arm in the direction Avram was pushing the raft.

"Thank God." The old man steered the door as well as he could in the direction the child indicated.

Miriam moved to the edge of the wooden planks. "I will help you push."

"Stay where you are. No." Avram tried to shout, but a lack of breath made his words emerge barely above a whisper. Before he finished speaking, the child was already in the water beside him. "Make sure the rope stays securely tied around you, little one."

Miriam imitated Avram's frog-like kicks to propel them forward behind their life-saving door. She was not much help with the pushing, but the removal of her slight weight made steering the raft easier.

After what seemed to be a long while, Avram turned his head toward Miriam. "Let me lift you back up. I need to see if we are going the right direction." He helped her scramble back onto the door and held onto a foot while she stood gazing into the distance.

“Yes,” Miriam said. “We are almost there.”

They waded ashore on an island narrow enough that Avram could see water both to his left and, more distantly, to his right. The terrain had a fair amount of vegetation on the hills that angled into the sea. The old man knelt and praised God for bringing him and Miriam to a place of refuge.

To his surprise, Miriam burst into tears.

“What is this?” Avram pulled her into a hug. “For a day and a night, you have been such a brave little girl. There is no need to start crying now that we are on dry land.”

Despite his attempt at comfort, Miriam continued to weep as if her heart were breaking. At last, she choked out a single word, “Ima.”

“John Simon is taking care of your mother.” He lifted his eyes to scan the horizon. “They may be on their way here right now.” He glanced toward the hills. “Or they may even be here waiting for us. And until we are with them again, I will take good care of you.”

“Do you promise?” Her tear-filled eyes searched his face.

“I promise.”

She trembled and looked away from him. “My father left one day and never came back.”

“I know.” He smoothed her hair with his fingers. “Rest assured, I will never do such a thing.”

Miriam gave him a wary glance, but the tears stopped.

“Is anyone here?” Avram shouted as loudly as he could. The only response was an animal’s ragged cry.

Avram pulled the makeshift raft well inland from the water. “We may find use for this door later.” As quickly as he could, he untied the ropes and wound them into two coils. He looped one coil over his shoulder and laid the other aside. “That bleating sound tells me there is a goat nearby. Where there is one, there will be others. Let us go and get some milk, little one.”

After several tries, Avram was able to capture a female goat and tie her securely. Miriam giggled when he shot a stream of milk into her waiting mouth. He chose the more dignified method of collecting milk in his cupped hand and gulping it down before it leaked away between his fingers.

“I must rest,” Avram told Miriam. “Then we will climb to the summit and see what we can see.” He stretched out on the ground, frustrated that catching one wild goat left him exhausted. For the second time in his life, he had unexpectedly become responsible for a trusting child. He prayed that he was up to challenge.

Following his nap, Avram beckoned to Miriam. She followed as he began to climb the highest hill.

When they arrived at the hill’s summit, Avram saw no tents or houses in any direction, no man-made clearings, no evidence of a cooking fire. “Do you see any ships?” he asked.

Before answering his question, Miriam climbed a small but sturdy tree. “Yes. Very far away.” She pointed. “Do you see it there?”

Avram squinted. Gazing in the direction Miriam indicated, he saw nothing but blue water melting into gray mist. “No, but my eyes are no longer sharp. If you can see a ship, the sailors can see this island.”

He pondered their situation while Miriam came down from the tree and stood by him.

“When the time is right, we will build a bonfire here, on the top of this hill,” Avram said, more to himself than to

Miriam. "We will pray for a passing ship to espy the smoke and come to investigate it."

Miriam looked up at him with questioning eyes. "But uncle, we have no coals for starting a fire."

Avram could not resist a chuckle. "Your mother carried a metal pot of hot coals with us when we made camp to speed things up. But a shepherd can make fire from nothing but wood if he has to. It is not easy, but it can be done." He gazed into the distance. "The ship you saw will be past us long before we would get a good blaze going. No, first we will make a large clearing and stack it with dry wood. There is much to do." He sighed, and repeated, "Much to do."

"Shall I begin hunting for sticks?"

Avram smiled at her immediate acceptance of his plans. *May my faith in the Almighty One's deliverance be so steadfast.* "Not yet, child. First, we must have a shelter and a pen of some sort for our she-goat. I do not relish the thought of chasing her down for her daily milking."

"Then you will not make the bonfire today?"

"No, not today." He stroked his beard. "Perhaps not for many days. "It may be that someone will come to harvest the wild olives or perhaps to take away a few goats before we need the bonfire. We will not depend on that, however."

Chapter Eleven

Channah opened her eyes and wondered where she was. Nothing in this room was familiar. Not the plush, fleecy pallet nor the soft blanket. Certainly not the beautiful, neatly-folded tunic lying near her feet. She heard the occasional murmur of female voices, though she could not make out any words. When she sat up, she felt as if she floated in restless water. The memories returned in a rush. The ship breaking apart, waves separating her from Miriam.

"Good morning." A pleasant-looking woman glided toward the bedside. "I am Salome. What is your name?"

"Channah."

"Well, Channah, Dorcas will be pleased to know you are awake."

She pulled the blanket around her neck to hide her nakedness. "Who is Dorcas?"

"The mistress of this house." Salome bent to smooth the bedding. "I will bring you something to eat. You must be starving."

"Where am I?"

"At the home of Dorcas, the clothier." She nodded. "She is the one who gave you these garments."

There were many other questions Channah wanted to ask, but she held her tongue. She was too hungry to delay receiving food.

As Salome's footsteps faded, Channah slipped out of bed and unfolded the tunic lying on top of her blanket. It appeared to be new, and made from very fine linen. Since her own clothing was nowhere in sight, she put the tunic on. She tied the belt loosely, but left the colorful coat and matching scarf on the bed. Why would someone she did not know give her such fine garments? Perhaps Salome misspoke.

Channah's eyes told her the house stood on dry land. However, her senses insisted the floor was bobbing with the rhythm of coastal waves. She leaned against a wall, which helped restore her equilibrium.

Salome returned, bearing a tray full of dishes. Another woman followed her.

"Good morning. According to Salome, your name is Channah. I am Dorcas. We brought you some broth and wine. How are you feeling this morning?"

"I am slightly dizzy," Channah answered honestly.

The two woman set bowls on a low table. Dorcas beckoned. "Come and eat. The sailors who brought you here said you took almost no nourishment the three days you were aboard their ship."

Doing as she was told, Channah sat on the floor near the table and stirred the clear broth in front her. Although she was weak with what she supposed to be hunger, the broth had the unappealing smell of sea water. She swallowed a sip, and then tried the wine. It tasted somewhat better than the soup, but the smell kept her from drinking very much.

She glanced aside at Dorcas's concerned face. "Forgive me. I do not seem to have much of an appetite this morning," she said.

Dorcas patted her hand. "Perhaps later. You have been through quite an ordeal."

Channah nodded. "I must go down to the place where the ships come in. I have to find my family."

Dorcas's eyes widened, but her voice remained calm. "The men who brought you here picked up seven Greek sailors and you."

"My daughter and my husband were not among them? Nor my great uncle?"

Dorcas caressed Channah's shoulder. "No, dear."

"No children?" Channah shivered. "No other passengers?"

"Not yet, but other ships may bring in more survivors in the next few days. I will keep checking. Meanwhile, you must regain your strength."

Channah did her best to eat, but soon gave up. "I cannot take more."

"Rest now." Dorcas stood and placed a hand on Channah's head. "Perhaps you will be hungry later. Salome will be nearby if you need her."

Channah found that walking calmed her churning stomach. She paced back and forth, often looking through the window that framed a view of the harbor. Surely, her loved ones would soon arrive. With that hope in mind, she was motivated to regain her strength. John Simon was never sick, but Miriam and Avram might need her to nurse them back to health after the ordeal of the shipwreck.

She spoke softly, "Salome?"

The woman appeared as if from nowhere. "Yes?"

"I believe I can take some nourishment now, if it is not too much trouble."

"No trouble at all." Salome's bright smile reinforced her words.

"May I go with you?" Channah asked. "That way you need not carry a tray."

"If you wish. Come along."

The broth that smelled of sea water that morning now tasted better than any food Channah could ever remember. She broke the small loaves of bread Salome sat before her, dipping chunks into the soup, and savoring every bite. "Is this an inn?" she asked.

Salome chuckled. “No, of course not. Whatever gave you that idea? This is Dorcas’s home. Her clothing business occupies part of the first level facing the street. We work and live in the other rooms.”

Channah ate more bread, realizing something she needed to make known. “I have no money at all. When my husband comes—”

“Dorcas expects no repayment,” Salome interrupted. “Even if you offered coins, she would refuse them.” Without asking, she refilled Channah’s soup bowl.

“Thank you. You are very kind.”

Salome smiled and patted Channah’s hand. “Kindness is one of our master’s commandments. You see, in this house, we are followers of the Way.”

Channah stopped eating. “You believe in Jesus?”

“Yes, Jesus of Nazareth, the one who was crucified and then miraculously rose from the dead. He is our promised messiah.”

“How amazing. My family and I are believers, also. That is why we are leaving Israel. A horrible man named Saul is arresting followers of the Way all around Jerusalem. Some have been killed.”

“Ah, yes, Saul of Tarsus. We have heard of him.” Salome made fists with her hands, but then relaxed them. “I know we are not to wish evil on our enemies, but this man makes that commandment hard to obey.” Salome stood. “If you require no more food, I will go and help the other women. Dorcas’s sheep produced a batch of wool that needs processing.”

Channah brightened. “Dorcas owns sheep?”

“Our mistress is a very astute businesswoman,” Salome smiled and lifted an eyebrow. “She has always raised flax for making linen. This year, she purchased a flock of sheep. She hopes to make a better profit by not paying the ever-rising prices of the wool merchants.”

Chapter Twelve

The cool, moist morning air continued to disagree with Channah. She hoped to eventually develop a tolerance to the unpleasant smell of the sea. Despite not feeling her best, she became restless for something to do.

Wandering into the spacious workroom, she observed seven women, including Salome, busy at various tasks. One picked burrs and twigs from the newly-shown fleece. Two others washed the cleaned wool, using sturdy sticks to stir the material in a vat large enough to bathe two people at once. From time to time, one of the stirrers removed the wet wool from the washtub and spread it on wooden racks to dry. Her partner refilled the tub with another batch of raw fleece. The other workers sat in a semi-circle on a brightly-colored carpet, combing and carding the clean, dried wool.

Salome looked up from her work and smiled. "Good day, Channah. I am glad to see you up and about. You must be feeling better. Come and meet the others." Although she tried, Channah knew she would not remember the names all at once. Their warm welcomes made her understand they would not be offended by her forgetfulness.

She saw a basket full of wool ready to spin. Something in her ached to find a spindle and start to work on the basket. She wanted to make herself useful. Also, she longed for an activity connected to the normal life she led before her world turned upside down. She listened for a time while the women chatted. Finally, she worked up her courage. "May I be of help in your work? I do not have any tools, but I know how to card and spin."

Salome's hands stilled. "Do you mean to say you know how to spin wool?"

"I have worked with it since I was a child."

"What a blessing," an older woman declared.

Another murmured, “The Lord sent her to us.”

“We know flax,” Salome admitted. “We’ve been putting off spinning the wool because none of us has ever done it before.” She put her work aside and stood. “We have plenty of spindles. Come and choose one.”

Channah looked through a basket filled with different sizes of drop spindles. She tried the balance of three before selecting one. The women crowded around and watched her begin to make woolen yarn from the carded fleece.

“You did not roll the wool on your thigh to get it started,” Salome commented. “We always do that with flax fibers.”

Although Channah was unaccustomed to being the center of attention, it felt good to demonstrate her competence. “I have never tried that method, but it would probably work. I just start the wool the way my Aunt Yael showed me.” Soon she was sitting on a stool and working alongside the other women.

“How did you lose your husband?” the woman whose name Channah remembered as Anna asked.

“I am not a widow,” Channah answered quickly. “My family was in a shipwreck, and we got separated. I am certain my husband and daughter and also my great uncle were picked up by a different ship than the one that brought me ashore. Any day now, I expect them to arrive back here.”

Several women sent furtive glances toward Channah. No one spoke for a long moment.

“Dorcas is kind to everyone,” Salome said at last. “But most especially to widows. She takes in women like me who have no family to look after them and pays us good wages. I would be begging or starving if not for her.”

"And she gives clothes to the poor." Anna stretched her arms before reaching for another handful of raw wool. "Why were you traveling on a ship? Are your family merchants?"

Such a thought made Channah smile. "No, we are shepherds, but we are also followers of the Way. A Pharisee named Saul has stirred up so much persecution around Jerusalem that we had to flee in fear for our lives."

"We have heard of this Saul," Salome said. "Do you remember, ladies? Simon Peter spoke of him when he was here."

"The apostle Peter was here?" Channah was surprised.

"Oh, yes. He has been preaching around the countryside for a while now. He and the other apostles decided he should stay away from Jerusalem for a time." Salome rose and tucked her carded wool into a big basket. Then she took more dried, washed wool and resumed carding. "There are rumors King Herod planned to have Peter executed, as James was. But an angel helped him escape from jail."

"But we are safe here," Anna said. "Dorcas will take care of us. Everyone in Joppa likes and respects her."

Channah concentrated on her spinning. She remembered how secure she felt in her tent before the trouble started. She hoped Anna was correct that persecution would not occur in Joppa. However, John Simon and Avram were convinced there was no safe place in Israel anymore for the people of the Way. Thinking about her family and the home they abandoned brought tears to her eyes. She struggled to keep them from rolling down her cheeks.

Dorcas swept into the room with the freshness of a spring breeze, carrying a large basket of food. "Good morning, ladies. Ah, Channah, here you are."

“Hard at work.” Salome gestured toward the spindle Channah had wound with a fine strand of wool.

Dorcas inspected the spindle hanging from Channah’s hand. “Very nice. This fine-spun wool will make up into an exceptional garment.” She turned the spindle over and over before allowing it to dangle again. She laid a hand on Channah’s shoulder. “I sighted a ship coming in to the harbor. I am on my way now to take food and see if the ship is carrying more survivors of your shipwreck. Would you like to come with me?”

“Oh, yes.” Channah laid her spinning aside and stood. “Thank you. Perhaps my family is on the ship. I am so looking forward to seeing them again.”

Dorcas handed Channah a stack of folded tunics. “If you would not mind carrying these, that will give me both hands to manage the food basket.”

Once outside, Channah could see that Dorcas’s home was situated on a high cliff overlooking most of Joppa, with an impressive view of the sea coast. Houses sat haphazardly along the downward-sloping hillside, none of them nearly as imposing as those perched on the bluff.

Dorcas led the way down a well-worth path. “How did you learn to spin wool so finely?”

“My aunt showed me,” Channah replied. “She and my uncle raised me. They taught me how to tend sheep, and working with wool was a natural part of what we did.” She glanced toward the port, where a vessel was docking. “I am hoping my Uncle Avram is on that ship, along with my daughter and my husband.”

“Salome tells me your family is leaving Israel because of the persecution.”

“Yes. We are followers of Jesus.”

"Then you are blessed, regardless of the hardships that have come."

Channah pondered Dorcas's wisdom as the pathway became steeper. In her urge to be reunited with her loved ones, she had not been particularly thankful for her own survival. All her prayers focused on the welfare of Miriam, John Simon and Avram. Had not John Simon told her Jesus warned his followers they would face difficulties in this life? She resolved to concentrate on being grateful for the kindness of Dorcas and the widows.

Widow. Did that dreaded word now describe her? *No, John Simon is strong. And he would never abandon Miriam or Avram. Yet I did. Unwillingly, tossed by the wind in the waves, that is what I did. I left my child alone to fend for herself in the sea. No, not alone. John Simon and Avram were there. And you, Lord Jesus. Your spirit is with them even now. I beg you to bring all three of them home.*

Channah remained deep in thought and silent prayer the rest of the way down the hill.

"Wait here with our things," Dorcas instructed at the place where the dock met the shoreline. "I will speak with the ship's captain."

Channah paced back and forth, constantly watching for anyone coming ashore. Finally, a figure appeared at the top of the gangplank. It was Dorcas. She waved an arm to beckon Channah to her.

She took up the food and clothing and walked as quickly as her burdens would permit. *Perhaps Uncle Avram is too weak to walk, or he may be injured.*

Dorcas met her halfway and relieved her of the heavy basket. "They brought in three gentiles only, no children. Probably these survivors are sailors."

Channah could not have been more shocked. She had been so certain her missing family members were aboard this ship. Her lips trembled. “My husband might possibly be mistaken for a gentile.”

“But how—” Dorcas’s puzzled expression faded to understanding. “I see.” She shook out the folded tunics and passed them to a nearby sailor. “These are for the survivors. They cannot come into Joppa in the nude.”

The sailor nodded, accepted the clothing, and went below.

Channah cast her eyes downward, not knowing what to say. She wondered if she would be banished from Dorcas’s household since her benefactor now knew her husband was uncircumcised. She fingered the fine tunic Dorcas had given her and realized she must have been naked when the strangers fished her out of the sea. She stole a sideways glance at Dorcas, who was sorting through the food she brought.

Three men climbed onto the deck from below. Channah could see at once they were young and strong, if somewhat haggard. Two of the tunics Dorcas donated fit well. The third hung loosely on the thinnest of the three men. John Simon was not among them.

Channah was relieved to find Dorcas did not refuse to help the shipwrecked sailors. Even though they were gentiles, Dorcas gave each one a bag of food. She asked if they needed shelter in Joppa, but all three indicated they planned to find employment on another ship. She blessed them in the name of Jesus before she and Channah left.

Chapter Thirteen

Dorcas came and sat beside Channah on the waist-high rock barrier between Dorcas's house and the edge of the cliff. The two of them sat watching the sunset without speaking.

"No more survivors have been brought in for weeks." This was information known to everyone in Joppa, but Channah felt the need to say the words. For more than a month, she had met every ship. "Most likely, they are dead. All three of them, swept away by the storm." Channah buried her face in her hands, willing herself not to cry. "Without ever having a chance to say goodbye."

"As believers, we know we will see our loved ones again. In Heaven, there will be no goodbyes."

Channah dabbed at her eyes. "I thank God for that hope. I know it should make me joyful, but..." She turned to face Dorcas. "Why did I not die with them? I have no reason to go on living."

"Who lives or dies is something only God himself has the right to decide."

The two sat in companionable silence while the sun's last dying rays shimmered across the calm blue water of the sea.

"When I was a young sea captain's wife," Dorcas said, "I feared something terrible would happen and Joseph would not return from his voyages. But so far, he always has. By the time our son bought his own ship, I was complacent. Because his father always came home, I assumed Asher would also."

Dorcas moved the arm she had around Channah and folded her hands in her lap. "They never found any wreckage of Asher's ship. No one from his crew ever came home. He was my only child." Dorcas sat quietly for a moment before continuing. "Eventually, I decided I would hurl myself over the edge of this cliff and die."

"But you did not."

"No," Dorcas agreed. "Joseph happened to be home at Passover, and so we went to Jerusalem. We stayed for Pentecost, and we heard the apostle Peter preach about Jesus. Joseph and I both became believers that day. Now I find purpose in following Jesus. I am blessed to have the means to help others."

Channah toyed with the end of her belt. "I thank you for trying to encourage me. Truly I do." She searched for the right words to express her feelings. "I feel so empty inside because I have lost everything, my family, my home, my sheep. Sometimes, even my faith seems to falter. Each new day I pray for a miracle, but to no avail.

"Prayer is an interesting thing." Dorcas swatted at an insect that had the temerity to land on her face. "The Lord gives us what we need, not necessarily what we want, and almost never in the way we expect. As for miracles, I believe they happen all around us. However, we do not recognize them because they come to us in surprising forms. Our God never runs out of creative ideas."

Channah sighed. "Thank you for your wisdom, Dorcas. Now that I think on it, I suppose it was a miracle that you took me in. I do not know what would have happened otherwise. I hope you know how grateful I am for what you have done for me."

"You are more than welcome to live in my home as long as you like." Dorcas's voice grew softer. "I do not want to give you false hope, but occasionally ships going away from Joppa pick up people who have been shipwrecked. I heard of one man who was taken all the way to Spain."

"Is that farther away than Ephesus?"

“Oh, yes, dear. Spain is much more distant.

As the twilight began to fade into darkness, Dorcas stood and extended a hand to Channah. “Shall we go inside?”

Chapter Fourteen

Unable to sleep, Channah slipped from her bed and paced. Perhaps the stuffiness of the room was the cause of her restlessness. She weighed the benefits of catching a night breeze against letting in the foul smell that assaulted her nose every morning. The stuffiness of the room persuaded her. She opened the shutters and gazed at the harbor.

The beauty of the sea at night took her breath away. The gentle glow of a full moon reflected across the water, spreading a dim light over the landscape. The only movement was a ship gently bobbing up and down as waves lapped quietly against the shore. Channah sat in the semi-darkness, praying, thinking, and wishing. Perhaps someday she, like Dorcas, would find some way to relieve the grief that cast its melancholy burden on her every move.

If her family was somewhere out there, under that buttery moon, they had no idea where she was. They could very well think her dead. The only place they would know to search for her was Ephesus. She knew she had to find a way to go there. She would be alone, with nothing and no one to rely on but her Savior. "You are enough," she whispered. "I will depend on you to make my pathway straight, Lord Jesus."

Channah went back to bed, feeling a peace she had not known for some time. She curled on her side and tucked a hand under her cheek, in her normal sleeping position. She awoke with a most unexpected thought assaulting her. She turned over and attempted to go back to sleep. How could she possibly have such a sudden, powerful craving for a pickle?

A craving? Her eyes flew open wide. How long was it since her monthly bleeding? It was at least three weeks before taking the sheep to the community pasture. And the nausea that dogged her mornings but disappeared near midday. Could it be?

Leaping from the bed, Channah examined her waistline. She thought she detected a slight thickening. Was it the result of sitting in the work room most of the day instead of walking through pastureland? She went to the window and lifted her eyes toward Heaven in thanksgiving. She shuddered to think how recently she wished the shipwreck had taken her life, not knowing there was another life involved, the one growing inside of her.

Channah watched from her window as the approaching dawn invited Joppa to awaken to a new day. She could only imagine how thrilled John Simon would be if he knew. She patted her stomach and shed tears of joy.

At daybreak, she hurried to the pantry in search of someone to share her news with, and still wishing for a pickle. She found Dorcas and Salome sitting at the work table that stood in the midst of the room where food was stored. “Good morning,” she said. “How are you this beautiful morning?”

The women turned surprised faces in her direction. “Good morning,” Salome replied.

“We are fine.” Dorcas gave her an appraising look. “And you?”

“I am feeling better than I have in a long time.” Channah could not help smiling. “Now that I know the cause of my upset stomach.” She went to the crock of vinegar and spices and fished a cucumber from the bottom of the crock. “Dear ladies, I believe I am with child.” She took a bite of pickle, still smiling, and wiping vinegar from her chin.

“I have suspected as much for a while,” Dorcas said, answering Channah’s smile with her own wide grin. “You have not had a female bleed since you came to this house more than a month ago." She came and wrapped Channah in a hug. "I am so happy for you."

"Yes," Salome added. "I thought you might perhaps be suffering from a disease, but decided it was more likely you were displeased to find yourself expecting."

"Displeased?" Channah was incredulous. "For years I have prayed to conceive. I thought I was barren. How could I be anything but grateful for this blessing?" She sobered. "I know things will be difficult, with no family to turn to and no husband to help me raise my child." She stopped for a moment to savor the sound of the words *my child*. "Do you know the psalm that goes, 'My help cometh from the LORD, which made heaven and earth'? My uncle used to sing that song after the sheep were settled for the evening."

Dorcas released her embrace. "In the short time you have been here, Channah, I have come to love you like the daughter I never had. I would be honored for you to consider yourself part of my family. We will give you whatever support you need, for as long as you need it."

"You are too kind." Channah felt tears forming.

Salome took a crock from a low shelf and sat it on the table. "You will find last year's pickles more agreeable than the fresh-made batch. I experimented with these. They are both honey sweet and vinegar tart. Try one and see what you think."

Although she had just devoured a large pickle, Channah eagerly took another. It had a strange but delightful mixture of flavors. "Delicious," she declared. She took small bites, savoring the treat.

Salome stood and smoothed her tunic. "I will go and fetch Asher's old cradle from the storage room. It will be nice to hear a child's laughter in this house again."

"Dorcas," Channah said, after Salome scurried away, "I appreciate your offer more than I can ever express. But I must go away, to Ephesus. That is where my husband and my uncle will look for me."

The older woman was silent so long Channah began to think perhaps she was offended. "What I mean to say—"

Dorcas interrupted her with a raised hand. "I understand, my dear. Certainly, you must go. But surely you realize you cannot travel right now. It would be too dangerous, both for you and for your child."

"You are right, of course." Channah folded her hands protectively over her stomach. "But as soon as possible after my baby is born."

"You will be a stranger, alone in a pagan culture, with an infant to care for. Do you realize how difficult this will be?"

"No. I only know my family may be alive, all three of them, somewhere. I must find try to find them."

Dorcas tapped her fingers on the table. "Then we must make a plan. Sometime within the next two years, my husband will be returning to Joppa. I will ask him to take you to Ephesus."

"On a ship?"

"Yes, dear. You cannot hope to walk to Ephesus alone with a nursing baby. Have no fear. My Joseph is the best sailor under the sun, and he has made his ship sturdy. You need have no fear of shipwreck with him as your captain."

Channah fell silent, knowing Dorcas spoke wisely. The thought of putting out to sea again was terrifying. However, attempting to make a long overland journey alone was impossible.

"You must be able to make a living. You are already good at processing fibers. I will teach you how to weave cloth and make garments. Also, you must learn enough Greek to conduct business." She pursed her lips. "Sophia is the best one to be your language teacher." She put a hand on Channah's arm. "You have a great deal to do in a short amount of time. I know you will work hard to prepare for your journey."

Chapter Fifteen

"Where are we?" John Simon lay exhausted on the sandy beach while the fishermen took care of the unconscious centurion and his injured prisoner.

The white-haired man shook his head. "What?"

Changing to speak Greek, John Simon asked, "What place is this?"

"Ah." The man nodded. "We have brought you to the Island of Cyprus. Why were you dragging these half-dead men along? Were you shipwrecked?"

"Yes." John Simon sat up, feeling renewed strength from the food and wine he consumed on the fishing boat. "We were bound for Ephesus, but there was a furious storm. Our ship broke apart, and I got separated from my family. Perhaps you have seen them? My wife, our little girl, and our elderly uncle?"

"No, we have seen only you and these two. One of whom you could have allowed to drown as far as I am concerned." The old fisherman spat in the direction of the centurion. "How long were you in the water?"

"I am not sure. Two or three days, perhaps four." John Simon rubbed his aching arms. "I lost track."

"My sons and I must get back to our boat. We have a catch to deliver, and our wives will be worried about us. There is a village not far from here, in that direction." He pointed away from the shore. "We will leave food and water for you." He lowered his voice. "I doubt the soldier will recover. We did what we could for his broken bones, but his insides may be bleeding."

"Thank you for your help." John Simon ate a dried fish while the fishermen returned to their rowboat. Before long, they pulled alongside their small vessel, hoisted the rowboat from the water, and sailed away.

The centurion groaned and opened his eyes. He made a motion as if to sit, but moaned and returned to lying on the sand. “What…” his voice trailed away on a dry croak.

John Simon knelt beside the centurion and offered him wine. “Drink this if you can.” The man grimaced when John Simon lifted his shoulders, but managed to drain the drinking crock. Returning him to a prone position as gently as he could, he handed him fishes and bread. “You need nourishment. Eat slowly.”

While the centurion ate, John Simon moved to the prisoner. The man accepted bread, mumbled “Thank you,” and ate.

John Simon sat between the two men and passed bread and wine to them until they indicated they were satisfied. The prisoner struggled to his feet.

The Centurion growled, “What happened?”

“We were shipwrecked,” John Simon replied.

“I know that, fool. Where are we now? And how did we get here?”

The prisoner curled his toes in the sand. Even though the soldier’s questions were not directed to him, he spoke. “I heard the fishermen say this is Cyprus. As for how we got here, this man saved our lives.” He nodded toward John Simon. “He tied us with ropes and dragged us through the sea until a fishing boat picked us up about dusk yesterday. You were unconscious most of the time.” He returned to a sitting position. “Both of us would be dead if not for his help. May I know your name, young man?”

“I am John Simon.”

“I surmise you are a Jew. I am Titus Alva Valeria, a citizen of Rome, and at the moment, the prisoner of Centurion Cornelius. We are in your debt.”

"What is this?" Cornelius pulled at the straps holding sticks to the sides of his right arm and leg. "Why am I bound?"

"The fishermen devised splints as best they could for your broken bones." John Simon replied. "You have quite a knot on your head, also."

Cornelius winced when he touched his head. With obvious effort, he managed to struggle to a sitting position. "Broken," he said after using his good left hand to examine his right thigh. Then he pointed at John Simon. "I compel you to remain with me until I am healed. You are responsible for making sure my prisoner does not escape."

John Simon cast an appraising glance toward the centurion. "You are in a poor position to start issuing orders." He drew a dagger from inside the neck of his torn tunic and began to trim his nails. "If your prisoner wants to get away from you, he can walk away. Right now. You cannot stop him and I will not."

Titus laughed aloud. "It is true what they say about you Jews being stiff-necked people. Why should I want to escape?" he asked when he recovered his composure. "I may be the black sheep of my family, but my brother will never permit me to be convicted of harboring a runaway slave. It would be too embarrassing for the Valeria family. Actually, I am rather looking forward to partaking of the pleasures of Rome again." He chuckled. "And Centurion Cornelius has been ordered to take me there."

"Clever words." The centurion scowled. "It is a well-known ploy for a prisoner to pretend cooperation until he finds his chance to break away." He faced John Simon. "I know how you conquered people feel about your Roman masters. Why are you waiting to kill me? Do it now and get it over with. If nothing else, dying will end the pain in my bones."

"If I wanted you to die, you would have drowned two days ago." John Simon glanced toward Titus. "Both of you." He put his dagger away. "I am a follower of Jesus. I do my best to obey his commandment to treat others as I want them to treat me."

Titus came and sat beside John Simon. "Do you mean Jesus of Nazareth, the Galilean who was crucified? You knew him?"

"I heard him speak, and I saw him again after he returned from the dead."

"I see." Titus arched his brows. "You people already had a temple with no god in it and a sea one cannot drown in. Once a week your give your slaves a day off, and now you have a prophet who endured crucifixion, which no one in the history of the empire has ever survived. Most peculiar, I must say."

"Jesus did not survive the cross." John Simon spoke with quiet confidence. "He died, was placed in a tomb, and then God raised him back to life."

"The man was a troublemaker," Cornelius muttered. "His followers stole his body and made ridiculous claims about his resurrection."

"He rose from the dead. I saw him. I know what I know." John Simon stood and dusted sand from his torn tunic. "I believe the best thing is for me to go to the village and bring help."

"No." After three tries, Cornelius gave up trying to get to his feet. He sat on the sand, red-faced and breathing heavily. "We have to stay together."

"I admire you for trying to stand," John Simon said after a moment. "As you can see, it is futile." He motioned inland. "Since we do not know how far away the village is, I cannot tell you when I shall return." He took a step away from the shore.

"I do not know that I am able to climb that cliff," Titus said. "I feel rather weak in the knees at the prospect."

"Stay here, conserve your strength, and take care of our friend." John Simon nodded toward the Centurion.

"Excellent plan." Titus settled just out of Cornelius's reach. "As it so happens, I have never cared much for long walks."

"Wait." Cornelius lifted his left arm. "What assurance do we have you will not desert us here on this godforsaken beach?"

"You have my word," John Simon replied. "That will have to be enough." He took another step. "Rest assured, the Spirit of God is here, even on this uninhabited strip of sand. Let us hope he saved you from drowning for a purpose beyond Cyprus."

The hill rising from the beach was steeper than John Simon anticipated. It took all of his resolve to continue climbing. Each time he felt his strength about to give out, he reminded himself that every step he took could be bringing him closer to Channah. She continued to be uppermost in his mind. He had spent most of the time in the water thinking about and praying for his family.

The sun was high in the sky when John Simon reached the crest. When he spotted a cluster of houses in the distance, he stopped to say a prayer of thankfulness. In addition to asking God to protect his family, he prayed to have patience with the two Romans for whose welfare he had unexpectedly become responsible.

***

"I doubted we would ever see you again when you didn't return yesterday," Titus commented when John Simon and three men from the village descended from the hill. "It appears we will be taking a hike. Alas."

Cornelius's face contorted into grimace as the men lifted him onto the litter, but he did not utter a sound.

"The villagers have a cart waiting on the other side of the hill," John Simon explained. "We will be able to follow the road to a town called Polis. From there, we can make our way to the seaport of Paphos."

"Oh my." Titus sighed. "That sounds like an arduous journey. Just climbing up this mountain you call a hill seems rather daunting. And then I suppose we must go down the other side."

"Yes," John Simon assured him. "You can stay behind if you prefer."

"No!" Cornelius moaned. "I must bring the citizen to Rome."

Titus rolled his eyes and began to move forward. "Enchanting as this little beach is, I fear it would be utterly boring to remain here alone."

It took a while for the men to struggle up and over the seaside ridge that separated the strip of white sand from the road. At last, John Simon guided the makeshift litter onto the bed of the large cart. Then he helped Titus climb aboard.

"These people call this a road?" Titus grumbled. "It is nothing more than a pair of ruts. No doubt we shall have a bumpy ride."

John Simon did not consider the complaint to be worth an answer. He thanked the two departing villagers for their help while patting one of the donkeys on her flank. "May I ride next to you?" he asked the driver. Taking the nod of the fellow's head to be affirmative, he swung himself onto the seat made from tree trunks. He could do without the company of the two Romans. However, his real purpose was to continue an earlier conversation with the cart's driver. The man appeared to be interested when John Simon told the story of Jesus in the village last night.

Chapter Sixteen

"You are wasting your time, young man," the dockside tax collector told John Simon. "Centurion Cornelius has made it clear that you are to accompany him and the citizen Titus Valeria to Rome. I do not expect an eastbound ship any time soon. Even if one comes in, I cannot allow it to transport you."

"I understand." John Simon tucked his thumbs in his belt and gazed toward the gently lapping sea.

"Take heart." The tax collector did not look up from the scroll unrolled before him. "Ships come and go every day from the port of Ostia, which serves Rome. You will have no difficulty going anywhere in the empire from there, provided you can pay for your passage. If not." He lifted his eyes and shrugged. "Roman roads are very good."

John Simon left the tax collector to his accounts and walked along the shoreline, thinking. There was no good reason for Cornelius to force him to remain with him all the way to Rome. His prisoner was clearly glad to be going home. Even if Titus was putting up a deceptive front, there was no practical way for him to escape while sailing across the open water.

He walked along, considering his options. He could hide somewhere until the ship bound for Rome left the harbor. Wherever and whenever he separated himself from the centurion, he would face the problem of earning money. At the moment, his possessions were his weather-beaten, torn tunic, the belt the cart driver gave him, and the fine dagger he tied to his body before the shipwreck. Selling the dagger would probably keep him fed for a few days, possibly a week. And then? The sensible course was to stay with his companions and pray for some form of deliverance in Rome.

John Simon retraced his route along the shoreline. From time to time, he stopped and scanned the horizon. Where in this great sea did the shipwreck send his wife? He fought against admitting she might be dead. No, Avram was with them. If necessary, the old shepherd would give his life to protect his niece and her child. If only there was some way for John Simon to know they were safe, and where they were. Surely, the God who saved those two irritating Romans would also have compassion on Channah.

Titus was scandalized when John Simon suggested passing the night in the open to avoid moving the centurion from the spot on the beach where the donkey cart left him. "Do you actually mean for us to sleep on the ground, in the open, with no shelter?" Titus demanded.

"Yes," John Simon replied.

Cornelius lay stretched out on the sand. "The earth is softer here than in many places where my soldiers and I have slept."

Titus stood with fisted hands on his hips. "This is unacceptable. I may be technically a prisoner, but I am also a Roman citizen."

John Simon settled into a sitting position, doodling in the sand. "No doubt there are inns in this port city, if one has the means to pay."

Whirling on the centurion, Titus shook a finger at him. "You are responsible for my comfort."

"I am responsible for getting you to Rome." He closed his eyes.

"I could go into town and find accommodations on my own." Titus pressed his lips together tightly.

"If you escape," Cornelius said, "I will have the Jew indicted, and he will pay the penalty for your crime."

"Have you no gratitude? This man saved your life." Titus seemed to be genuinely shocked.

"As a Roman soldier, gratitude is an emotion I cannot afford." The centurion moved slightly and winced. "I have a duty to perform."

Titus sat a short distance away. He pressed his hand on the sand. "I am certain I cannot sleep a wink without a bed." When neither John Simon nor Cornelius responded, he muttered, "My family will be outraged at my treatment."

John Simon lay staring up at the stars. He understood now that he was to be Cornelius's scapegoat in the event Titus did make a getaway. *I could easily slit both Romans' throats in their sleep and tow their bodies out to sea.* As soon as that thought occurred to John Simon, he prayed to be forgiven of it. He asked for strength to follow the Way of Jesus, regardless of the cost.

The next morning, John Simon awoke at his usual time, just before sunrise. Titus lay on his back, mouth open, snoring loudly.

When he saw the centurion was awake, John Simon asked, "Did you rest well?"

"I did not chance going to sleep after my unguarded words of last night. I expected you to slip away in the night. Or perhaps do something worse." Using his left arm for support, Cornelius struggled to a sitting position. "You are not the first follower of the Way I have encountered. You are an unpredictable lot, most peculiar."

"We are commanded to be kind."

"No, it is not that which sets you apart in my mind. I have observed many people who treat others generously." Cornelius turned his head left and right, and then rubbed the back of his neck. “You seem to have no fear of death. How can that be?”

“God promises eternal life to those who believe in his son, Jesus. He demonstrated his power over death by raising Jesus to life after his crucifixion.” After a short silence, John Simon continued, “Like every man, I want to live. I have a family that needs me. So, I do not seek death. Neither do I fear it. Whenever my time comes, I will rely on the words from the Psalm, ‘Even though I walk through the dark valley of death, I will fear no evil, for God is with me.’”

“With you?” Cornelius glanced around. “I see no one here but that noisy patrician.” He nodded toward Titus.

“He is here.” John Simon tapped his chest. “His spirit lives in the heart of the believer. I felt him with me strongly during the shipwreck, and all of our time in the water.” He cocked an eyebrow. “If not for the Spirit’s prompting, I would have saved only myself and left you and Titus to fend for yourselves.”

“Why should your god be interested in whether or not I drown?”

“He created you. He knows your name. Why he chooses to love you and me is a mystery I do not understand. But he says he does, and that is enough for me.”

The centurion’s words took on the familiar mocking tone. “The emperor, whom I faithfully serve, claims to be a god.”

“What emperor ever walked out of his tomb, taking up life after death?”

“You are perilously close to speaking treason,” Cornelius warned.

Suddenly there was an exceptionally loud snort, Titus jumped, and his eyes flew open. “What was that horrible noise?” He sprang to his feet. “It must have been a wild animal.”

“What you heard was your own snore.” John Simon caught Cornelius’s grin before it disappeared.

“That is impossible.” With a wide yawn, Titus declared, “I have not slept at all.”

“Are you going to help me get Centurion Cornelius to the ship?” John Simon asked.

“Oh, I am most willing.” Titus put a hand in the small of his back. “Unfortunately, however, I have a weak spine. It is an old condition that flares up from time to time. My physician has warned me I must not risk an injury.”

Chapter Seventeen

John Simon and two dock slaves carried the centurion to the row boat that would take them to the ship anchored in the harbor. Titus walked behind, ignoring Cornelius's instruction for his prisoner to remain in his field of vision.

John Simon leaned near the soldier's ear. "He is not going anywhere. He is only trying to annoy you."

"I have my orders," Cornelius muttered. However, he did not speak to Titus again. Once on board, he inclined his head toward starboard. "Stand me up over there. I will lean against the side of the ship."

Recognizing the futility of argument, John Simon backed to the opposite side of the deck. He and the sailors put Cornelius on his feet beside a waist-high wooden railing. For a moment, it appeared the centurion would collapse. He gripped the rail with whitened knuckles, and swayed against the bulkhead.

John Simon placed a wooden stool behind Cornelius. The soldier grunted what might have been an expression of thanks and eased onto the stool. "This will do."

Noticing that Titus was empty-handed, John Simon returned to the beach to fetch the last of the food the villagers gave them. The stale bread was better than nothing.

When he returned to the ship, Titus sidled up to him. "You will never be able to get Cornelius down that rope ladder." He gestured toward an open hatch that led to the lower deck.

"I have no plans to attempt to take him down there." In response to Titus's questioning look, John Simon added, "He will have to sleep topside, where I will remain also."

“I did not realize you were so attached to our soldier friend, that you cannot leave his side for the evening.”

“One shipwreck was enough to convince me to avoid the lower decks, especially in the dark.”

“Oh.” Titus’s fleshy face went slack. “I never thought about that.” He peered over the side of the ship. “But surely your god will protect us from another disaster.”

John Simon could feel warmth flooding his face. “Do not make light of the Lord God Almighty.”

“I shall endeavor not to do so.” Titus flashed a smile that did not reach his eyes. “Anyway, I doubt the quarters down below are any more accommodating than this deck, and most likely they are not clean. Perhaps I shall join you and the good centurion on deck this evening.” He frowned. “Even though we have no shelter.”

John Simon turned and walked away to allow his anger at the Roman to cool. He leaned across the wooden rail and watched Cyprus slowly disappear from sight. He wandered around the deck and talked with some of the sailors. Although he rarely slept during the daytime, he decided to curl up behind the containers of olive oil stacked on the deck. After a long, leisurely rest, he awoke and began to stroll around again. He found two sailors engaged in deep conversation. Wandering nearer, he realized they were discussing the next day’s weather. “I do not like the look of those horsetail clouds,” the younger sailor said.

The older man turned his wrinkled face skyward. “Yes, we may be in for some trouble. I think not tonight, but tomorrow.”

“Is a storm is brewing?”

“Could be,” the old sailor replied. “This is an unpredictable time of year. The signs will be clearer in the morning.”

The men stopped talking and stared at John Simon. He nodded a greeting and walked on as if he had not heard their words. He went and leaned his arms on the rail. The sky revealed nothing to him, but he knew experienced sailors were able to predict the weather based on cloud formations. He gazed at the azure sea, sparkling and rippling in the sunlight. It was hard to imagine such a tranquil scene turning malevolent. Yet, he knew only too well how quickly a fierce wind could trouble the waters.

He caught a movement in the corner of his eye. Cornelius had pulled himself to a standing position. The centurion took two small steps before returning to sit on his stool. Although he resented all Romans, John Simon respected Cornelius's dogged determination to overcome his injuries. It was a favorable comparison to Titus's self-centered complaining. What a pair.

"Channah, where are you?" John Simon whispered into the breeze. "Do you know I will never stop searching for you?" He dropped his head and prayed for his absent family. After a while, he straightened and wiped the tears from his eyes.

The evening passed quietly. The following morning, John Simon noticed the wind gradually whipping up. He wandered around the ship, speaking about Jesus to any sailor who would listen.

By midday, a dark cloud obscured the sun. The wind continued to increase, and growing swells rocked the ship.

No one uttered the fearsome word 'storm'. As the wind increased, no one spoke all. John Simon helped Cornelius move his stool to a more protected spot out of the rain that began to pelt the deck. Then he made sure his dagger was securely tied to his chest. He sat on the deck near the ropes that secured the ship's one small rowboat, hugging his knees.

"Here he is." Titus yelled. "I have found him."

When John Simon lifted his head, raindrops stung his face. The citizen's expression bespoke fear.

"Please." The ship's captain elbowed Titus aside and shouted over the howling wind. "Will you pray to your god to spare us?"

John Simon considered the captain's request. His prayers normally consisted of asking for strength and courage to face whatever trials came his way. He was not sure the Lord would entertain a plea to calm a storm to save a bunch of heathens. "I will ask," He shouted into the captain's ear. "I cannot say what he will do."

"You must try." For once, there was no sarcasm in Titus's words, only desperation. "You are our only hope."

Chapter Eighteen

John Simon followed the captain to the center of the deck, fell to his knees, and lifted his hands toward Heaven. He prayed urgently for the ship to hold together, for the storm to subside, and for everyone aboard to survive. He repeated Psalms of comfort and protection, asking the Lord Jesus to demonstrate his power and bring the heathen crew to belief. After some time, he realized the rain was not striking him with so much force. The ship still rocked, but no longer violently. Feeling an unexpected warmth, he opened his eyes. A single shaft of sunlight pierced the breaking clouds and bathed him in its warming light.

He and the sailors who gathered around him watched the storm cloud move away from them, leaving behind a clear sky and just enough wind to fill the sails.

After a long period of silence, the captain put an arm around John Simon. "I have never known a man with such power."

"The power is not mine," John Simon assured him. "It is all God. He commands the wind and the waves, and they obey his will." He brushed rainwater from his hair. "We would do well to follow their example."

In the following days, some of the sailors attributed the passage of the storm to random good fortune. Others peppered John Simon with questions about the teachings of the Way whenever there an opportunity.

After rounding the Island of Sicily, the ship followed the coastline to Rome. John Simon slept more soundly knowing land was in sight for the remainder of the voyage.

One evening, the captain announced the ship would dock at Ostia sometime the following day. Titus sat near John Simon against the ship's rail, their backs to the water. "What will you do when you reach Rome?" the citizen asked.

"I must find work." He fingered his tunic. "This garment is about to fall apart. And, of course, there is the little matter of eating." He shrugged. "As soon as possible, I want to go on to Ephesus."

"Is that your home?"

"It was, once." John Simon hesitated. Titus had discontinued his sarcasm since the storm. Still, it was not like him to take an interest in someone other than himself. "I was separated from my family when we were shipwrecked on our way to Ephesus. My prayer is that I will find my wife, our daughter, and my wife's uncle there."

"What is your wife's name?"

"Channah." John Simon visualized her face. "It means grace."

"Lovely name."

"She is a lovely woman. Her name suits her well."

"I had a nice wife," Titus volunteered. "She left me. I cannot say that I blame her. I treated her like a slave."

Water lapping against the ship's bow was the only sound for a moment. Finally, John Simon asked, "Are you worried about your trial?"

"There will be no trial. My brother will call in a favor or bribe a senator, and the whole thing will be forgotten." He stretched out his legs. "Not that it matters, but I am not guilty. It is just one of life's little ironies I suppose, that I have done much evil but not the thing I have been legally accused of."

The men sat in silence for a while. John Simon sensed there was something more the Roman wanted to say. He waited patiently.

Titus stood and, turned his face toward the sea before speaking. "I am forty years old. I have never cared for anyone or anything other than myself. As a young man, I pursued pleasure relentlessly, until it no longer brought me any satisfaction. These last few years I have felt so empty." He paused and leaned on the rail. "For the first time, I have hope there is more to life than wine, women, and fine horses. Not only did you save my life, you have given me much to think about with your constant talk of your god. I am in your debt."

Before John Simon could speak, Titus hurried away without so much as a backward glance.

The ship docked at mid-morning. John Simon stood alone and heard the captain advise everyone to wait while he cleared his cargo. Titus handed the captain something—John Simon could not see what it was—and then the captain walked away briskly.

With the aid of a broomstick, the centurion hobbled to the port side of the ship. Titus was nowhere in sight, but he would not be able to disembark without passing by Cornelius's watchful eye.

When the captain returned, John Simon approached him. "I cannot pay for my passage," John Simon said. "May I help unload the ship?"

"No doubt the dock slaves will welcome your assistance." The captain hurried away without further comment.

John Simon worked hard, despite the sweltering heat. He hoped his labor made up somewhat for his inability to pay for his passage and the food he consumed while on board. With the last of the barrels of olive oil sitting on the dock, he did not feel guilty accepting a ration of moldy cheese and wine with the other men.

John Simon called out when he saw Cornelius lurching forward, "Let me help you." He put an arm around the centurion as the soldier attempted to walk down the gangplank.

Titus appeared. "Wait." He stepped in front of Cornelius, turned toward him, and steadied him by putting his hands on either side of the centurion's waist. Together, the three of them managed to negotiate the steep incline.

A well-dressed man came striding toward them. "Greetings, Titus Valeria," he said.

"Sixtus." Titus clapped the man on the shoulder. "How good of you to come. I hoped my brother would receive my message. How are things at the estate?"

"Everyone is quite well, sir."

"I see you brought the large chariot."

"Those were my instructions." The man glanced toward Cornelius. "Shall I take you home now, sir?"

"Yes, but we are not going directly to the villa." Titus inclined his head toward Cornelius. "First, we will stop by the military barracks, where Cornelius and I will check in with the tribune. He needs assurance the centurion brought his prisoner home to Rome." He stretched out a hand. "You brought the other thing?"

Sixtus handed a pouch twice the size of a fist to Titus, who opened it and stirred the contents.

The citizen closed the pouch and thrust it toward John Simon. "It is a long walk to Greece, my friend, over some formidable mountains. My suggestion is to take this money and get on a ship headed east. Anywhere it goes will take you closer to Ephesus than you are now."

Feeling the shape and weight of coins in the bag, John Simon was puzzled. "I do not understand."

"I feel you deserve a reward for saving my life." In a softer tone, Titus added, "Perhaps in more ways than one."

"I did not pull you out of the water for money."

"If I thought you did, I would give you nothing." Titus turned toward his servant. "Bring the chariot closer, Sixtus, and then I will need your help to get the centurion aboard."

He took Cornelius's arm. "After we do our business at the barracks, perhaps I should introduce you to my physician."

John Simon watched as the chariot pulled away with its passengers. When he opened the pouch Titus gave him, he was shocked. It contained several gold aurei, each worth 25 pure silver denarii, along with numerous other coins of varying denominations. Grateful for his unexpected blessing, he decided to take Titus's advice and sail east as soon as he bought food for his journey and twine to repair his tunic.

Chapter Nineteen

Channah hummed the tune of a psalm as her shuttle flew back and forth across her loom. Dorcas had patiently taught her various patterns of weaving. As soon as she mastered one assignment, Dorcas showed her something even more intricate and beautiful.

"Lovely," Sophia commented.

"Thank you," Channah replied. She was no longer frustrated by Sophia's rule that she was to speak only Greek during the day, since she now knew a great many words and how to use them. She was not as fluent as her teacher, and doubted she ever would be. Nevertheless, she was able to conduct business with speakers of Greek.

Dorcas poked her head into the weaving room doorway. "I am going to the travelers' encampment this morning, Channah. I was wondering if you would be interested in accompanying me?"

"I would be more than happy to do so." Channah was always glad to take a break from weaving and go places with Dorcas. Throughout Joppa, people recognized her and treated her with respect.

Channah secured her twine, marked her pattern diagram, and pushed her loom against the wall before going to join Dorcas in the courtyard. The donkey cart stood waiting, filled with provisions.

"We are delivering food this morning," Dorcas said cheerily. "Then we will take a side trip to visit my little flock of sheep."

Her words brought a smile to Channah's face. The delight Dorcas took in giving gifts was contagious. Plus, it had been too long since she had felt the wooly warmth of a lamb.

Dorcas handed the reins of the cart to Channah. "I do not understand why, but this donkey behaves so much better when you drive."

Channah guided the cart through the courtyard's side gate. She often visited the stable before the workday began, stroking the little donkey and feeding her treats. She waited while Dorcas closed the gate and climbed back into the cart. They drove past the grand houses perched on the cliff, making their way through open country to the camp where refugees waited to escape persecution.

Those at the campsite were not the same people Channah met when her family stayed there. Yet somehow, it was as if nothing had changed. Various sizes of temporary shelters sat around the perimeter of the field. There was now a well-worn pathway leading toward the well. She sat for a moment, lost in her memories.

Channah put a hand on her belly. As she had so many times before, she wondered where John Simon was this morning. Was he tending sheep with her uncle somewhere near Ephesus, with Miriam working and learning beside them? Thoughts of her loved ones came to her at unexpected times, sprinkling the salt of sadness over the joyful anticipation of welcoming a son or daughter into the world.

"Are you all right?"

The sound of Dorcas's voice cleared thoughts of the past from Channah's mind, at least for the moment. "I was thinking about my family. In some ways, it seems only yesterday we arrived at this camp. Then again, it feels almost like a different lifetime."

Dorcas patted her hand. "I understand. I was uncertain about bringing you here for fear of painful memories."

"It is fine." Dorcas's cart sat low to the ground and had a step suspended from the side. Channah moved slowly to descend from the driver's seat. She rested with an arm tucked behind her back while men from the camp unloaded the provisions.

Dorcas visited with the group of women who stood exclaiming over the food they were receiving. Channah hung back. Her natural reticence was not the only reason. The women were bound to ask questions. She did not want to discourage these hopeful travelers with her story of shipwreck and loss. After a while, she went and rubbed the donkey's ears. "You did a good job, pulling the cart this morning," she whispered. "Notice how happy everyone is to see that the Lord has provided them with plenty of food." When her protruding belly bumped against the donkey's neck, she smiled. "See, not all is lost. I will soon have John Simon's baby to love."

When the provisions Dorcas brought had been distributed, she returned to the cart. "Shall we go?"

Channah nodded, gave the donkey a handful of grain, and climbed aboard. Dorcas directed her to a pasture not far away. "These are my sheep," Dorcas waved a hand toward the flock. "I do not see the shepherd, but surely he is nearby. I am hoping to gain more profit by shearing my own sheep. Fleece gets more expensive every year."

Without waiting for an invitation, Channah climbed from the cart and slowly approached the nearest ewe. The animal needed grooming. Her hooves were untrimmed and gnats swarmed around her ears. Channah wandered around, inspecting the listless sheep. When she returned to the cart where Dorcas sat waiting, she was almost in tears.

"Their coats should thicken up nicely over the next few months." Dorcas seemed to be oblivious to the condition of her animals.

Silently, Channah climbed to the driver's seat. She sat holding the reins of the cart, not knowing how to inform Dorcas about what she had observed. At last, she took a deep breath and said, "Your shepherd is not worth his hire."

In response to Dorcas's surprised expression, she went on, "The sheep are not being cared for. One of them already has a badly infected leg. If changes are not made immediately, hardly any of your sheep will live until Spring."

"I had my doubts about the man I hired," Dorcas looked around. "At the very least, I expected him to be with the flock."

"Do you have a sharp knife with you?" Channah asked.

"I do. Why?"

"I can begin trimming the sheep's hooves."

Dorcas stared at her in obvious disbelief. "My dear, that sounds like hard work. Perhaps it is better for me to go to the marketplace and search for another shepherd to engage."

Channah hesitated. Dorcas was a skillful businesswoman, but she obviously knew nothing about raising sheep. Was it rude for the student to instruct the teacher? Nevertheless, something had to be done because animals were suffering. "These poor sheep need attention now." She alighted from the cart. "Let me take care of them until you find a good shepherd."

"How may I help?" There was no resentment in Dorcas's tone.

"I need olive oil for their ears, and wine to treat cuts and scratches." Channah stopped and thought for a moment. "A measure of grain and a walking stick.

Perhaps some rags, a large crock, a razor, and four arm lengths of rope."

"Surely you do not mean to stay out here in this pasture by yourself?"

Channah could not keep herself from smiling. "I have been alone with only my sheep more times than I can count." There were small houses within sight, making her doubt she would encounter a wolf or a bear. If the necessity arose, she could use her belt as a makeshift sling.

"I will send my stable boy with food and your supplies as soon as I arrive home." Dorcas flicked the reins over the donkey's back.

Chapter Twenty

When Channah awoke in the middle of the night, she realized it was time for her baby to be born. She decided to stay in bed until sunrise. No doubt Salome and Dorcas would chide her later for not awakening them immediately. However, she had delivered enough lambs to know that it might be a while before her son or daughter was born.

Between contractions, Channah thought about names. For a girl, she had chosen Yael, in honor of her beloved, deceased aunt. She was still torn about the name for a boy. Although she wished to honor her husband or uncle, she was reluctant to reuse a living person's name. Sophia spoke Greek names in a way that was most pleasant to the ear. Convinced her child was to be raised in Ephesus, she wondered if she should heed Sophia's advice. Her Greek companion suggested giving a male child a name that did not immediately identify him as a foreigner. She tried to get comfortable while mulling over names for the hundredth time. Nicholas? Alexander? Something with a Roman sound, perhaps Marcus?

Although she hoped not to awaken anyone, a sharp pain caused her to cry out. Before long, Dorcas was by her side. "I will send for the midwife," she said. "Salome will bring her in the cart." She began to massage Channah's legs and arms. "By this evening, the pain will be gone, and you will hold your babe in your arms."

She held onto that thought as the contractions began to come closer together. The midwife lived nearby, but it seemed to Channah as if it had been a long time since Dorcas sent for her. She felt as if she was drowning in a sea of pain.

"The baby is coming fast," the midwife said as soon as she examined Channah. "Quick." She motioned to Salome. "Help me get her up and onto the stool."

Channah cooperated with the midwife's instructions. Soon, she felt the child emerge from her body, accompanied by a scream she could not control.

"The midwife lifted the bawling baby and smiled. "A boy," she announced.

After the midwife tied and cut the umbilical cord, Channah collapsed onto the bed. The midwife wiped her hands and turned to Salome. "Mix me a solution of honey with olive oil and salted barley water. I will bathe the child before I go."

The baby stopped crying when the midwife placed him on his mother's chest. Although she was exhausted, Channah was eager to see if he was deformed in any way. She cuddled him close to her with one hand and used the other to bring his tiny hands and feet into view.

"He is perfect." Dorcas sat next to the bed and put her hand lightly on the baby's back. "Have you decided on a name for your son?"

"My son," Channah repeated. The words touched her already melting heart. "Joshua. I will call him Joshua." She felt as if she could weep for joy. Instead, she fell asleep.

The next day, Channah spun wool while Joshua slept.

"You do not need to work," Dorcas chided. "Just take care of your baby."

Channah did not argue, but she did continue to work on the stack of prepared fleece. She did not want to take unfair advantage of Dorcas's generosity.

After a while, Channah began to suspect the other women were avoiding the wool. Then she heard Sophia mention the flax fibers were longer and easier to spin into an evenly textured thread. Channah was surprised, since the wool felt natural to her. It was the flax she found awkward. The group shared a hearty laugh. Then they decided each woman should choose the material she felt most comfortable working with.

The days passed pleasantly, with Joshua becoming the darling of the household. “It is good you make an abundance of milk,” Dorcas said as she handed the baby to Channah. “This boy is always hungry.”

She nestled Joshua in her arms and offered her breast to him. “He has to hurry and get big and strong to be ready to travel when Captain Joseph comes home.”

“Yes, I suppose so.” Dorcas sounded as if her words had no thought behind them.

After Dorcas left the room, Sofia leaned toward Channah. “She is not herself lately. Have you noticed?”

Although she had detected some unexplained difference in Dorcas, she did not want to say so. “How do you mean?”

Sofia shrugged. “I cannot say exactly, but I sense something is wrong.”

“Perhaps she is concerned about her husband. She told me a month ago she was expecting him to arrive in Joppa any time.”

“A few months is nothing in a sailor’s itinerary. Ships cannot sail all year. They have to stay in the nearest safe harbor when the winter months come.” With a glance away from her loom, Sophia repeated, “Itinerary. It means a traveler’s schedule. Now you have learned another Greek word.”

Channa shifted Joshua to her other breast. “How long has the captain been gone?”

“On this voyage? Let me think.” Sophia tightened a warp string on her loom. “It must be almost two years. I know he left before Simon Peter visited us.”

“Someone mentioned once before the apostle has visited Joppa. Do you think he will return someday?”

“Perhaps. He teaches all around the countryside, never staying too long in one place. His wife told me she fears for his life when they are in Jerusalem.” Sophia stopped weaving and turned to Channah. For the first time, Sophia spoke their native language instead of Greek. “You must go and hear him the next time he comes through. I have never heard a man speak with such power, such passion.”

Channah lifted the now-sleeping Joshua to her shoulder and gently patted his back. “My uncle Avram spoke highly of the apostle. I would love to hear his teaching whenever his *itinerary* includes Joppa.”

Sophia chuckled. “You are a quick study.”

Cradling Joshua in her arms, Channah hoped to be in Ephesus before Simon Peter returned to Joppa. She would gladly sacrifice the opportunity to hear the apostle’s teaching to be where she hoped and prayed to find her family. “He will be so proud of you,” she whispered into Joshua’s dark curls.

“Peter?” Sophia questioned.

“John Simon,” Channah replied. “This little man’s father. We will be reunited with him in Ephesus. Soon, I hope.

Sophia passed her shuttle back and forth, weaving the weft threads into the warps. After a long moment, she said, “What will you do if your husband is not in Ephesus? Will you come back to Joppa and be content?” She shifted her eyes sideways toward Channah for a brief moment. “Surely you realize Dorcas loves you and Joshua deeply. It will break her heart when you leave her house.”

“I must go and find my husband and my daughter. And Uncle Avram.”

“Channah.” Sophia stopped her work again and laid a hand on Channah’s arm. “It is a miracle that you survived a shipwreck. There is very little likelihood the rest of your family were also spared. You must consider the probability that you are now alone, with a child to raise and no one to help you. Dorcas is willing, even eager, to become the family you need. Think what you are throwing away by insisting on going to Ephesus.”

She knew Sophia spoke out of concern for her welfare as well as Dorcas’s feelings. Yet, something deep within Channah refused to give up the hope of reuniting with her loved ones. “I will pray for guidance toward the right path.”

Chapter Twenty-One

"Are we going to drag more fallen branches to the top of the hill today?" Miriam asked.

Her cheerful question twisted Avram's heart. "Not today, little one. I am not certain of the day, but we will celebrate the Sabbath starting today and every seventh day thereafter." He sat up and rubbed his eyes. Although he had spent most of his life living in a tent and sleeping in open pastures, the ground seemed to be getting harder.

"Shall I go and milk the goat?"

"Yes. That is a good idea." Avram stretched his arms and rubbed his neck and shoulders. In truth, he declared this day to be the Sabbath out of fatigue as much as a wish to honor God. The shallow limestone cave was little more than an indentation in the side of a cliff, but it provided them adequate shelter.

Discovering goats made Avram think someone lived on the island at some time in the past. The dust-covered remains of a campfire and a worn-out cooking pot confirmed his suspicions. He hoped the previous inhabitants would return, perhaps to harvest fruit from the several fig trees growing not far from his shallow cave.

After chanting his favorite psalms, Avram concluded with his daily request. *Oh Lord Almighty, nothing is beyond your power. Knowing this, I ask that you send someone to return Miriam to her loving parents. Only you know where we are, and only you can guide some ship to this shore. You know all things, my father. Therefore, you are aware that my strength is failing. You see how my heart races when I climb a hill or walk too far. I ask that you give me the strength to take care of this sweet girl and extend my life long enough to see her rescued. Please, in your mercy, do not leave her to die alone in this deserted place. Bless my beloved Channah and John Simon, and comfort them with the assurance their child is alive and well.*

"I found a big limb near the goat pen," Miriam announced as she came into the cave. "I wanted to bring it with me, but I was afraid the milk would slosh out of the hole in the cooking pot if I tried to hold it with one hand. Is it all right to drag branches to the hilltop on the Sabbath?"

"The Sabbath is a day to take enough rest that you can spend extra time adoring God. Right now, you must practice your psalms and say our prayers. Afterward, you may do whatever you have energy for. You should understand, this is not a strict application of the Law of Moses the way I learned it as a boy, but Jesus brought us freedom from the law."

"Abba told me keeping the Sabbath is one of the ten commandments."

"Yes, that is correct. Very good."

Miriam wrinkled her brow. "But were the commandments not given with the law?"

"Yes, child. I see you have been paying attention to John Simon's teaching."

She was quiet for a long moment before asking, "If Jesus freed us from the law, why do we keep the Sabbath?"

"That is a good question." Avram took a twig and scratched at the soft earth of the cave floor. "Perhaps it is to stop and remember that he rose from the dead. Also, in his wisdom, he knows our bodies need a day of rest after six days of work." He laid the stick aside and shrugged. "Beyond that, I do not know."

Miriam nodded, seeming to accept his response. "Abba told me questions that begin with 'why' often have no answer."

"Even though he is young, John Simon is one of the wisest men I have ever known."

After Miriam's lesson and prayer, Avram released her. "You have done well, child. Now you may go and do whatever amuses you for as long as there is daylight. Be sure to be back here before sunset."

"Yes, Uncle." Miriam jumped up and stepped outside the cave's wide mouth. "How many more dry branches do we need before you set the signal fire?"

Avram pondered her question, yet another one for which he had no definite answer. "The Lord will show us when to light the signal." He stroked his beard. "We must have a clear day, so the smoke is visible. If you should happen to spot a ship in the distance, run and tell me. When you can see a vessel, its sailors should be able to see our fire."

"Will you make fire from two sticks, the way you did before?" She gestured to the campfire crackling just outside the entrance to the cave.

"No, by the time I got the fire going, the ship would have passed by. I have a long, sturdy branch set aside. We will light it like a torch from our campfire and hasten to the top of the hill where the wood for our signal fire is set."

"And then a ship will come for us."

"I hope so." *If the torch does not burn out on the way up the hillside. If the fire gets going before the ship passes. If we do not accidentally start a forest fire. If the sailors are observant. If we are not picked up by rogues who will kill me and sell the child into slavery. If God smiles on us.*

"You will see. Abba says God hears our prayers, and I pray three times every day for a ship to come to this island." She smiled and skipped away.

"Oh, to have such faith," Avram said aloud. He considered going to add to the pile of dry wood he and Miriam had been gathering. Instead, he leaned against the cool wall of the cave and went to sleep.

The sound of Miriam's voice awakened him. "Uncle, you have almost let the campfire go out."

Avram rubbed his eyes, struggling to remember where he was. "Campfire?" he repeated. He sat trying to clear the confusion from his mind while Miriam added kindling and stirred the coals. When a tiny spark appeared, she blew on the kindling to tease the campfire back to life.

"Good job." He stretched and shook his head, still trying to think clearly. "Thank you for reviving the fire. I would not relish having to start from scratch to make a new one."

Miriam added some larger chips of wood, eventually returning the fire to a full blaze.

"Tell me, how did you know how to rekindle the fire?"

"From watching Ima." The girl continued to poke at the burning wood.

"Did you also pay attention when I used the sharp stick and the notched log to start the fire?" he asked.

"I saw what you did."

"Tomorrow, I will teach you to make fire."

Miriam's face wrinkled into a frown. "Now that the campfire is burning well, there is no need to make new fire."

Avram leaned forward and rested his hands on his bent knees. "It is important for you to learn how to do things for yourself." When the child did not speak or glance in his direction, he added, “In case there comes a time when I am not around.”

Almost whispering, she said, “You promised you would not leave me.”

“And I never will,” Avram assured her. “Not willingly. But I am an old man, Miriam. Sometimes old men go away, even though they do not want to.”

“When are you going?” Will it be soon?”

Avram stretched out his legs and held out his arms. “Come and sit on my lap.” When she did so, he wrapped her in his arms. “As long as God gives me life and strength, I will do my best to take care of you.”

“My first abba left and never came back. Then my first ima left me, too.”

“I know.” He laid his cheek on the top of her head. “Your natural father made a decision I will never understand. Your mother was different. She did not wish to die, but when her appointed time came she had no choice. However, you see how God provided Channah and John Simon to become your new parents. Someday our family will all be together again, that I can promise.” It did not seem to be the right time to reveal that the someday he spoke of might be in Heaven.

Miriam buried her face in his chest and wept. “You are very kind, Uncle,” she said between sobs. “But I want my ima.”

Chapter Twenty-Two

A few weeks later, a woman Channah did not recognize burst into the weaving room. "Where is Dorcas?" the woman demanded breathlessly.

"I am Dorcas." The voice came from outside the doorway.

"Please come to the camp right away. A woman is trying to give birth, but she is having trouble. She may die."

Sophia secured her shuttle and stood. "I will fetch the midwife."

"Yes, do," Dorcas agreed, stepping into the room. "And ask the stable boy to hitch up my donkey cart. Channah, will you drive me?"

Following a whirlwind of activity, Channah handed Joshua to Dorcas and climbed into the cart beside her. After making sure the messenger woman was seated in the cart bed, she gently flicked the reins and spoke to the donkey. The animal instantly broke into a fast trot.

"I do not understand how you manage to communicate with this donkey," Dorcas muttered. She pulled Joshua's blanket closer around his face. "You love to go for a ride, do you not?"

"He seems to enjoy motion and speed, like his father."

They arrived at the camp ahead of the midwife. The woman who had brought the message leapt from cart before it was fully stopped. "This way." She motioned toward a ragged tent.

Although she was not certain she recognized the suffering woman on the bed, Channah spoke the name "Lora?"

The pale-haired woman opened her eyes briefly. "You know me?"

Channah knelt beside the straw pallet. "We were in the camp together last year. I am Channah, the wife of John Simon."

"Ah, yes. I remember now. You gave us your cart and donkey. How kind of you to come. You were not able to complete your journey either?"

"We were shipwrecked."

"Oh, I am so sorry." Lora turned her head toward Channah. "We were attacked by bandits on the road somewhere north of Syria. My husband was killed." A great sob burst from deep within her throat. "When I awoke my children were gone. The robbers must have thought I was dead. Some spice traders returning from Persia brought me back here, to Joppa." She groaned.

"Oh, my dear." Channah wiped Lora's tears. "Rest now. You are about to bring a new life into the world."

The midwife crowded into the tent and wedged herself between Dorcas and Channah. Without any conversation, she pushed back the thin blanket and felt of Lora's stomach. She stood and motioned toward the outside.

Channah followed Dorcas outside the tent, dreading what she feared the midwife was about to say.

"The woman is not in good health. I doubt she will survive. It is best if I crush the child's head and bring it forth immediately."

"No." Channah put a hand on the midwife's shoulder. "You must not kill the baby."

With a shrug, she answered, "It will die anyway. The mother is too weak to nurse it."

“I will take responsibility for the child,” Dorcas answered.

“I have plenty of milk,” Channah volunteered. “I will be the wet nurse.”

The midwife’s eyebrows shot skyward. “Do you not understand? That woman is a gentile. Her baby is an unclean thing. I would not have come if I had known.”

Dorcas’s voice was strong. “Both mother and child are human beings. If they die, we will accept God’s will. Until he makes his choice known, we will do everything we can to save their lives. Go your way if you wish.” She turned toward the tent. “Come, Channah, we have work to do.”

“You need not go outside and whisper,” Lora said when the pair re-entered the tent. “I know I am dying. My only prayer is to summon enough strength to give life to my child first.” She lifted a hand. “Please find someone to take good care of him. I ask you in Jesus’s name.”

“We will.” Dorcas jiggled Joshua in her arms. “I promise.”

While the messenger woman held Joshua, Channah and Dorcas delivered Lora’s child. They wiped the tiny, whimpering baby girl clean and put her into Lora’s arms.

“You have a beautiful daughter,” Dorcas said.

“Thank God.” Lora whispered. “I would like for her name to be Julia, to honor my mother. I pray she will follow the Way.”

When she realized Lora was no longer breathing, Channah took baby Julia in her arms. It took some maneuvering to feed Joshua and Julia at the same time, one nursing at each breast. Meanwhile, Dorcas made arrangements to pay a family from the camp to anoint Lora’s body.

“Poor little orphan.” Dorcas nuzzled Julia after taking her from Channah. “She makes Joshua look like a giant.”

“She is tiny,” Channah agreed. “Perhaps Lora did not carry her to full term.” She glanced toward the tattered tent where women from the camp were already gathering. “Should we stay?”

“No.” Dorcas moved toward her cart. “They will take care of the body. We need to get this baby properly bathed and warm.”

Dorcas drove the cart home, with Channah holding the two infants. At the entrance to the courtyard, Dorcas called out for someone to open the gate. The stable boy came on the run. He stood open-mouthed when Channah handed him a baby to hold while she got down from the cart.

Emerging from the house, Salome quickly came forward to take the newborn from the stable boy. She smiled and cuddled the baby close. “We never know what will happen when Dorcas comes home from one of her mercy missions, do we?”

Before long, Salome had the child bathed and wrapped in a soft new blanket. The women sat in a comfortable corner of the weaving room. Salome and Dorcas carded wool while Channah fed the two babies again.

“You can take Julia now,” Channah said. “She has quit nursing and I think she is falling asleep.”

“Julia? That is an odd-sounding name.” Salome reached for the tiny bundle. As she re-wrapped the baby’s blanket, she asked, “Shall I go into town and look for a wet nurse?”

Without lifting her eyes from her work, Dorcas spoke softly. “I doubt you would have success.” In response to Salome's questioning look, she added, "The child is a gentile."

"What shall we do with her, then?"

Channah noticed Salome no longer cuddled Julia close.

Dorcas's voice took on a sharper tone. "I promised a dying mother I would take care of her child. That is what I intend to do." She took the baby from Salome.

"I have plenty of milk for two," Channah said in the awkward silence following Dorcas's revelation.

Both Salome and Dorcas seemed to ignore Channah's words. "But, Dorcas," Salome began.

"I made a vow, Salome. This baby must be raised in the Way. Whether she lives as a Jew or a Greek does not matter."

"Think what you are saying," Salome insisted. "It is one thing to forsake our old customs for the Way. I recognize we should be kind to everyone, even foreigners. But to welcome a gentile into your *house*?" She gestured toward Channah. "Sucking at her breast? Someday eating at your table? What will Captain Joseph say?"

Chapter Twenty-Three

Channah sat in the sun-lit pantry nursing Julia. She tried to feed the baby girl when Joshua was asleep or otherwise occupied. Her son was making progress toward being weaned. However, anytime he saw Julia nursing he wanted to join her. "I am saddened that Salome is leaving us," Channah said to Dorcas.

"Let her go in peace," Dorcas advised. "She has found employment serving a wealthy household nearby. God willing, she will find her way back to us after she has time to settle her mind."

"She is going away because of Julia, I fear."

"Yes, probably." Dorcas put pots and plates away in the open shelving.

Channah shifted Julia from her right to her left breast. "How can someone take offense at a sweet little baby?"

Dorcas came around the table and side hugged Channah. "Salome has a good heart. We will see her at the weekly worship. And I know she cannot resist coming to hear the Apostle Peter when he comes back through Joppa."

"Salome has always been kind to me," Channah allowed. "Are you expecting Peter to visit any time soon?"

Dorcas shrugged. "Travelers show up whenever they can."

Channah wondered if Dorcas was thinking of her sea captain husband as well as the apostle. Her little son was crawling and beginning to talk. She expected to have him fully weaned very soon. When that was done, she was determined to make her way to Ephesus. She lost herself in thought while Julia finished nursing. What was her family doing in Ephesus today? She had no doubt John Simon was taking good care of Miriam and Uncle

Avram. Were the three of them somewhere on a sunny hillside this morning? Perhaps they spoke of her as they tended their sheep. *Holy Spirit,* she prayed, *reassure them I am alive and will come to them as soon as I can.*

Channah realized Julia was no longer nursing. She adjusted her clothing, put the baby on the floor on a blanket, and began to punch down the day's portion of dough.

Bethel appeared in the doorway. "Look who woke up." She sat Joshua near where Julia lay.

"I will be in the big work room for a while." Dorcas announced. When Joshua crawled after her, she laughed and picked him up. "Do you want to learn to weave, little man?"

Joshua replied with the word he used more than any other. "No."

"Do you want to stay here with your ima?"

"No," Joshua replied, causing the women to laugh.

Dorcas picked up the boy. "Come with Bethel and me, then."

Channah knew Dorcas and the other women would look after Joshua while she shaped her dough into loaves.

Julia lay quietly on the pallet, her eyes following Channah's every move. She stretched her arms forward and very plainly said, "Ima."

Channah grabbed up the child. "Your first word! Yes, I am one of your imas." Although she knew Julia mimicked Joshua by referring to her as mother, hearing that word from the baby touched her heart. She cuddled Julia and nuzzled her fuzzy little head.

"Come quick! See if you can help." Anna's frantic words broke into Channah's thoughts.

"What happened?" Receiving no answer, Channah dusted flour from her hands.

"Dorcas fell." Anna sank to the floor weeping.

"Where is she?"

"In the big work room. Hurry."

"Watch Julia." Channah rushed to the work room, concerned not only for Dorcas, but her own little boy.

Channah wove her way through the group of women. She scooped Joshua into her arms and knelt beside Dorcas.

"I must have fainted," Dorcas whispered. Her eyelids fluttered. "I think I hit my head."

"Yes, you did." Bethel was at Dorcas's other side, holding her hand.

After assuring herself Joshua was not injured, Channah let her wriggling son loose. He quickly crawled to his favorite toy, an old cooking pan filled with clean stones too large for him to swallow. He spilled the stones on the floor and began dropping them noisily inside the pan, an activity he never seemed to grow tired of.

Turning back to Dorcas, she asked, "Can you walk enough to get to your bed?"

"Maybe. If you help me." Dorcas slowly sat up. "I just sat Joshua on a blanket. When I stood up, I felt strange. The next thing I knew, I was lying here and someone was asking me if I was all right."

"Have you fainted before?" Channah asked.

"No, never. Not even when I was pregnant." Dorcas lifted a hand to touch the back of her head. "Ouch."

As gently as she could, Channah felt the spot where Dorcas's fingers rested. "You already have a knot.

That is good. My uncle says it is better for a head to swell out rather than inward."

With Channah and Bethel helping, Dorcas stood. "I feel so peculiar," she said.

"Do you want to wait a while before you try to walk?" Bethel asked.

"No." Dorcas set her jaw and leaned heavily on Channah. "Just help me get to my room, please."

Once inside her chamber, Dorcas collapsed onto her bed. Her voice was barely audible. "Thank you. I should be all right in a while."

Channah was not convinced. Her friend's skin was pale, and her eyes had a faraway look that frightened her. "I will send for a doctor."

"Yes. A doctor. Good." Dorcas closed her eyes while the women spread a thick blanket over her. "I must sleep now."

Channah motioned for Bethel to follow her. Outside Dorcas's chamber, she stopped and rested a hand on Bethel's forearm. "Stay with Dorcas. Try to keep her from going to sleep. I will bring the doctor as soon as I can."

In response to the woman's quizzical expression, she said, "I do not know why, but my Uncle Avram says it is not good to sleep immediately after a head injury. He is not a physician, but he has a lot of practical healing knowledge."

Channah returned to the work room. "Has someone gone to fetch the doctor?" she asked. Her question was met with blank stares.

"Is that what you want us to do?" a woman with tears streaming down her cheeks asked.

"Yes," Channah replied. "Immediately. Who knows where to find the doctor?"

After a long silence, someone said, "Salome knows."

In an uncomfortable instant, Channah realized the women expected her to be the group leader. She took a deep breath. "Tell Anna she is responsible for the babies. Everyone else, stop working, go to Dorcas's chamber, and pray fervently for her. God willing, I will return with a physician soon."

Channah ran to the stable, where the attendant helped her hitch the donkey to Dorcas's cart. "Do you know where to find a doctor?" she asked.

"No," the boy replied, wide-eyed. "Is someone sick?"

"Dorcas." She forced her mind to slow down and consider what to do. "Where is the home where Salome is now working?"

He pointed. "Five houses down the road leading to the shore."

Chapter Twenty-Four

Channah was relieved when Salome herself answered her pounding on the fine home's courtyard gate. "Salome, Dorcas needs a doctor. Please tell me how to find him. None of the other women know."

"Dorcas?" Salome cocked her head. "She is never ill."

"Today she is," Channah insisted. "She passed out, and we do not know why. Please, Salome, I must hurry and find a physician to attend to her."

Salome stood motionless, staring at Channah for a moment. "You would never be able to find the man Dorcas needs." She stepped outside the doorway. "I will give you directions as we go."

"But your employer..." Channah hurried after Salome, who was already striding toward the cart.

"Straight ahead," Salome said as Channah climbed onto the seat and gathered the reins. "We will turn toward the water at the first opportunity."

After many twists and turns, Salome instructed Channah where to stop. Without explanation, Salome leapt from the cart and hurried to the house's entrance where she spoke with the young man who came to the door. Returning to the cart, she reported, "The doctor knows where Dorcas lives. He will come as soon as he can."

"Why not now?" Channah asked.

"The doctor was up late last night with a patient. His servant said he will come as soon as he has finished his morning meal." Salome cut her eyes toward Channah before fixing them straight ahead. "Please take me to Dorcas now."

They rode through the city in silence, except when Salome indicated when and in which direction to turn. As

Channah guided the donkey onto the clifftop road, she asked, "Do you want to stop and speak with your mistress?"

"No." Salome adjusted her scarf. "Either she will understand or I will be out of a job." She twisted her hands together before speaking again, quietly. "I still do not approve of the gentile baby, but Dorcas has been so good to me."

"She is good to everyone. I will keep Julia away from you as much as possible."

"Thank you." She wrung her hands again and stared at them. "It is not that I wish the child any evil. I have let go of so many old ways, but it is hard for me. I am sure you understand."

In truth, Channah did not understand. However, Dorcas's revelation of Salome's strict upbringing under the Mosaic law gave her some insight into the older woman's position.

As soon as the stable boy opened the side gate to the courtyard, Salome stepped to the ground and hastened into the house.

Normally, Channah helped to unhitch the donkey, but on this occasion she left that to the stable boy and followed closely behind Salome. Inside the house, everyone was in Dorcas's chamber, crowded around her bed.

She was surprised to see Dorcas sitting up. When Joshua toddled toward her, Channah picked him up and kissed him. "Were you a good boy for Anna?"

"No," he answered solemnly.

Everyone laughed, including Dorcas.

"The doctor should be here soon," Channah announced.

"Yes, so Salome told us." Dorcas smiled. "I am feeling all right. Perhaps there is no need for the doctor."

Channah did not feel compelled to argue, since a chorus of women disagreed with Dorcas before she could speak. Instead, she motioned to Anna. "Please come and help me feed the babies."

As soon as they were away from the chamber, Channah said, "I am so glad to see Dorcas feeling better."

"Yes," Anna agreed. "She is almost her old self again. And she was very happy to see Salome."

The noise of hooves on the paving stones announced the arrival of the doctor's chariot. Channah made sure her bosom was covered while Anna ushered the physician inside. Rather than wait for Joshua's slow crawl, Channah took him in her arms and led the way to Dorcas's chamber.

"Doctor Marcus, how good of you to come." Dorcas spoke Greek, making Channah wonder if the physician was a foreigner. "I had a fainting spell, but as you can see, I am much better now."

With a wave of Salome's hand, the women began to exit the room. Channah turned to follow, but a staying hand stopped her. "She will want you to remain," Salome whispered.

Salome held her hands out to Joshua. "Do you want to go and play in the courtyard?"

Joshua willingly leaned into Salome's arms, despite saying, "No."

Channah pressed her back against the wall, expecting to be told to leave. However, neither Dorcas nor the physician seemed to notice her.

"I am not certain what happened." Dorcas spoke with a shaky voice. "I suppose I must have tripped over something, but I am fine now."

"When you struck your head, did that hurt?" he asked.

Dorcas looked puzzled. After a moment, she answered, "No. Actually, I do not recall hitting the floor. I was walking along, and the next thing I remember is someone asking me if I was all right."

"I see." The doctor stroked his beard. "Then it is more likely you passed out and that is what caused your fall. Can you walk now?"

"Certainly." Dorcas swung her legs over the side of the bed. She stood, but quickly returned to a sitting position. "I am slightly dizzy. Give me a moment." She rested her forehead in a hand.

Instantly, Channah went to Dorcas's bedside. "Do you want me to help you?"

"No," the doctor said. "I want to see what she can do on her own."

Channah stepped back, while Dorcas took a deep breath and stood.

"Now walk." The physician extended his hands without touching Dorcas.

After a tentative step, she fell into his waiting arms. With his help, she sat on the side of the bed again. "I am not as strong as I thought." Without further comment, she stretched out and closed her eyes. "Maybe I need more sleep."

Channah watched as the doctor squeezed Dorcas's arms. He spread her fingers and examined them one-by-one. Then he felt of her neck and head.

The doctor turned toward Channah and smiled. "It is a bad humor. It will pass. She must remain in bed for five days. Keep the room quiet and dark."

The women waiting outside the door did not react when the doctor repeated his diagnosis and instructions to them. They filed silently back into Dorcas's bed chamber. Stepping outside the doorway, Channah spoke to Salome. "Thank you for helping me find the doctor. I would never have been able to locate him without you."

Without acknowledging Channah's thanks, a grim-faced Salome said, "I fear there is more to Dorcas's illness than the doctor told us. I have a bad feeling about this."

Channah shared Salome's reservations, but did not speak of them.

That evening, some of the women slept sitting against the wall of Dorcas's bed chamber. The others stretched out on the floor around her bed. Sometime during the early morning hours, Dorcas stopped breathing.

"But we prayed," Bethel protested to anyone who would listen.

Chapter Twenty-Five

Channah was sitting in the courtyard feeding the babies when Salome came outside to sit beside her. She turned to Channah and asked, “What are we going to do?”

“I sent Anna and Bethel for the spices and ointments we need. We have already moved the body to the upper room. I suppose—”

“That is not what I mean,” Salome interrupted, holding up a hand as if it helped to stop Channah’s words. “There are orders to fill, materials to purchase, deliveries, food to buy. So many things.” She swiped a hand across her forehead. “If only Captain Joseph were here.”

“But he is not.”

“No,” Salome agreed. “Alas.” She began to weep. “I cannot believe she is gone. It all happened so fast. How are you going to take care of the women?”

“How am *I* going to take care of them?” Channah was not certain she heard the question right.

“Without the livelihood Dorcas provided, the widows will be homeless and hungry.” Salome glanced toward Channah before drying her eyes. “You are the nearest thing to a relative poor Dorcas has. Had, I mean. If someone does not step in soon, there are evil men in Joppa who will take everything before Captain Joseph gets home to stop them.”

“But the government—”

Salome laughed without amusement. “They will be the first to steal from a dead woman with no family to prevent them.”

Channah pondered the situation. “How I wish my husband and uncle were here. They would know how to safeguard Dorcas’s possessions for the captain. I am not acquainted with such matters, but I know enough to realize men who would turn widows out into the street will not listen to any mere woman. Is there not one honest man who might be willing to help? What about Dorcas's neighbors?"

Salome shook her head. "They only tolerated Dorcas because they admired her charity. They disapproved of her following the Way of Jesus." She twisted the end of her scarf in her fingers. "When I was child, we would turn to the rabbi, but these days they are as bad as the Romans when it comes to widows and orphans."

Salome dabbed at her eyes. "If only the Apostle Peter were here. I know he would help us. I hear he is in Lydda. Perhaps he will come to Joppa before the vultures strip Dorcas's house clean. Lydda is only a half day's journey away."

"Maybe the Apostle could send someone to Joppa to help us." Channa grasped Salome's forearm in response to an idea that struck her. "We must go and ask him."

"Who would carry the message?" Salome asked. "As I said, Lydda is a half day's journey from here. Even if you and some of the widows were to go in search of him, women alone on the road would never reach their destination. You would be robbed and probably worse as soon as you were beyond shouting distance." She resumed her weeping. "We are without hope."

"There is always hope in the Lord," Channah insisted. "That is something my uncle taught me from my childhood."

For a long moment, Channah considered the situation. She had taken no wages from Dorcas, only room and board. The understanding was that Captain Joseph's ship would take her to Ephesus when he returned to port, in payment for the work she had done. If Dorcas's possessions were confiscated, she would have no means of support and no way to get to Ephesus. She rubbed the dark curls atop little Joshua's head.

"I will go to the refugee camp and ask some of the men there to go to Lydda for us," Channah announced. "While I am gone, you must promise to care for my babies as if they were your own." Channah searched Salome's face.

"May God deal with me ever so severely if I do not do as you say." Salome reached for Julia.

Channah put the child into Salome's waiting arms. For an instant, she felt the older woman stiffen. Then, just as quickly, the rigidity disappeared. Channah hugged and kissed Joshua. "Be a good little man and do whatever Salome tells you. I will return as soon as I can." She trotted toward the pantry to pack some food.

"You cannot go to the camp alone," Salome called after her.

Channah ignored the admonition. The stable boy was no protection. He was still a child. The widows would only slow her down. She quickly gathered a bag of provisions, grabbed her cloak from a hook on the wall, and hurried back to the courtyard.

"Bethel may have the strength to walk to the camp and back," Salome suggested half-heartedly.

"She has gone with Anna to get supplies for anointing Dorcas's body," Channah reminded Salome. "It makes no sense to waste daylight waiting for her to return. And you know as well as I that Bethel has an ailing back." She stopped long enough to caress Joshua one more time. Her last words as she unlatched the gate were, "Take good care of the children and pray for me."

As she strode along the road to the camp, Channah removed the traveling cloak and tossed it around her shoulders. Despite the sadness of the day, it felt good to be out in the fresh air instead of laboring at a loom or spindle. Her thoughts took her back to happier days when she and her family quietly shepherded their herd in the Bethlehem hill country. Perhaps such times lay ahead of her, in Ephesus. Without Dorcas's support, how was she going to reach that far-off destination?

At the refugee camp, Channah spoke with the first person she encountered. "Shalom, my brother. I am here to find some men who know how to settle an estate. Failing that, I am asking for someone to go to Lydda and confer with the Apostle Peter. Is there anyone in the camp who can help me?"

"I will ask around," the man replied. Wait here and rest while I speak with the brethren." He put his head inside the nearest tent and spoke words Channah could not discern before moving on. Almost immediately, a woman emerged from the tent bearing a small tray of fruit and cheese.

Knowing food was scarce among the refugees, Channah took as little as she could without being impolite. She kept her eyes on the man going from tent to tent, praying he would find someone to assist her. She was encouraged when she saw the man turn back toward her, with a young couple following him.

"There are no educated men among us," the man said as he approached Channah. "This is Elias and his wife Rebecca. Elias has agreed to go to Lydda with me."

"Thank you." Channah noticed Rebecca walked with a noticeable limp, but Elias appeared to be fit. Channah told them of Dorcas's death, and commissioned them to find Peter and ask him to send someone to Joppa to help with her estate. "I brought this for your journey." Channah handed Elias the bag of food she had hastily gathered from Dorcas's pantry. To her delight, the men set out for Lydda immediately. She made a mental note to send a cart full of food to the camp as soon as she could.

A band of two men was small, but stood a far better chance of a successful journey than a group of women. She prayed for them all the way back to Dorcas's house.

Chapter Twenty-Six

John Simon could hardly contain his excitement as the port of Ephesus came into view. All memories of his hard work and deprivation faded into the joyful anticipation of seeing his family again. Now that he was finally at his long-awaited destination, he felt awkward. How had Channah fared? Perhaps after all this time, she believed he drowned in the shipwreck. Was Uncle Avram trying to convince her to take a new husband? He shook his body to chase those alien thoughts away. She would never give up on him. Not his Channah. If she was alive, she was waiting for him somewhere, taking good care of their adopted daughter and her old uncle. When would he be able to hold his wife in his arms once again, banishing all doubtful terms such as 'if' and 'somewhere' from his vocabulary.

The day was pleasantly warm. He had already served notice he was leaving the ship's crew at Ephesus. His wages were in the leather pouch hidden from sight inside his tunic. He leaned against the deck's low wall and seriously considered jumping overboard and swimming to the shore. He smiled to think how peculiar he would appear, walking through the city soaking wet. Difficult as it was, he forced himself to wait until the ship docked. He acknowledged goodbyes from his fellow sailors as they helped the dock slaves unload the ship's cargo of animal pelts and building stones.

Finished with everything he felt he should do, John Simon stood on the beach and wiggled his toes in the dark sand. He tucked his sandals in the bag slung over his shoulder and made his way up the gently sloping road.

The city seemed at once familiar and strange. He remembered carts hawking their wares along the road to the port. However, there seemed to be more of them now, and a variety of merchandise was being offered, though still mostly food. The smell of fresh bread caught his attention, but he knew prices would be better at the city's main commercial area. More importantly, he wanted to speak with locals. He expected Channah and Avram were working in the fields outside the city. He was hopeful that someone in the Jewish community would know where to find the shepherd family from Bethlehem.

At the hill ahead shaped into a natural amphitheater, John Simon turned right. He did not recall the marble street extending this far from the center of town. The new paving must have been laid during the years he lived in Israel.

John Simon noticed there were no beggars on the main thoroughfare, unlike many of the ports he visited in the last two years. No doubt that spoke to the prosperity of the city where he was born. There were also many more houses than he remembered on the hillsides surrounding the commercial developments. The Ephesus he had known as a child felt at the same time familiar and unknown. Even the Greek being spoken all around him had a different sound.

When he reached Curetes Street, he turned to his left toward the commercial market. He thought he remembered a synagogue in that area. He crossed the road to stay as far as possible from the slave market. He disliked the form of slavery practiced in Israel. He found the Roman system harsher and even more objectionable.

As he strolled along, he saw a Roman soldier coming toward him in full uniform. The crest on his helmet identified him as a centurion. Out of habit, John Simon ducked into the nearest shop doorway to avoid encountering the soldier.

"Good morning." The shopkeeper greeted him heartily. "Do you wish to place an order?"

Rows of idols lined the shelves that filled the back wall of the shop. "No, thank you," was his breathless answer.

"Well, then, perhaps you are interested in a household goddess. As you can see, we offer only the finest of figurines."

At that moment, the centurion John Simon saw on the boulevard strode into the shop. "Is my armor ready?"

"Yes, sir," the shopkeeper replied. "Let me get it for you."

John Simon slipped out of the shop as soon as the centurion's back was turned. He melted into the crowd, not stopping until he put some distance between himself and the metal shop. The smell of fresh bread drew him to a bakery where he purchased a hot, crusty roll topped with toasted sesame seeds. "Is there a synagogue near here?" he asked after savoring a bite of his bread.

The man's dark eyes bored into John Simon. "Why do you ask?"

"Someone at the synagogue may know the whereabouts of my family."

"Are you a Jew?"

"Yes," John Simon answered, although the question was debatable. With a Jewish mother and a Roman father, there were many who would deny his identity with either group.

Armed with the baker's directions, John Simon set out for the synagogue. Once there, he loitered across the narrow street. He had learned that approaching one man was safer than going inside. Some synagogues in the ports he had visited were tolerant of proclaiming Jesus as Messiah. Others banished him from the congregation as soon as they found out he followed the Way. In

Alexandria, the rabbi beat him with rods for blasphemy before throwing him out.

An elderly man emerged from the synagogue doorway, bent forward at the waist and leaning heavily on a cane. John Simon fell into step beside him. "Excuse me, sir. I have just arrived in Ephesus. The ship I was on broke up in a storm on our way here. I was separated from my family. I am hoping someone here has seen them and can tell me where they are."

The old man stopped walking. He glanced at John Simon, cupped an ear, and then continued hobbling up the road.

"My wife's name is Channah. She is about your height. Our little girl is almost as tall as my wife, though she would only be nine years old by now. They are with our uncle, a big man with broad shoulders, white hair, and a leathery face. Have you seen them?"

"What?" The old man shouted loudly enough to cause two women walking down the street to stare.

"I am searching for my wife." John Simon explained again. "Have you seen or heard of an elderly shepherd from Bethlehem, arriving with his niece and her daughter sometime in the last year or so?"

The man shook his head. Yet, when John Simon turned to walk away, the old fellow grasped the sleeve of his tunic. "Come," he yelled. After winding their way into a residential area, the old man rapped on a door. He smiled and nodded toward the doorway.

In response to a voice from inside, John Simon's unlikely companion belted out one word at top volume, "Mordecai."

Amid the sound of bolts being unlocked, a young voice complained, "There is no need to raise your voice, Grandfather. I can hear. *You* are the one who is deaf."

The young woman swung the door open. She seemed surprised to see John Simon. “Come in, please.”

The old man shuffled inside first. “Call your mother,” he shouted. “This fellow needs to find a wife.”

The young woman immediately disappeared through an interior doorway, either not hearing or not paying attention to John Simon’s saying, “I believe your grandfather misunderstood what I said.”

He turned toward the old man. “I am trying to find my wife.”

“Have no worry, young man.” The old fellow shouted, while patting John Simon’s arm. “My daughter is the finest matchmaker in Ephesus.”

The young girl who answered the door led a woman with an older version of her same face into the now crowded vestibule.

“Greetings. I am Thalia. Oh, my, you appear to be young and strong. Some fortunate woman—”

“Excuse me.” John Simon his hands in front of his chest, palms out. “I fear there has been some miscommunication. You see—”

“Ah,” Thalia interjected smoothly. “There is no need to be embarrassed. Many young fellows such as yourself come to me for help. Some because they have no father to make a choice for them. Others—”

Since Thalia continued to speak without ever taking a breath, John Simon interrupted her again. “I am married.”

“Well.” Thalia rolled her eyes toward her daughter. “That does complicate matters somewhat. Nevertheless, for the right price—”

“No. Please. I do not want a bride. I have one, and she is the only one I will ever want.”

Thalia's eyebrows lifted. "Then why are you here?"

It was a good question. John Simon wondered the same thing. "I was a passenger on a ship from Joppa. There was a storm, and the ship broke apart and sank. In the confusion, I got separated from my family, and it has taken me almost two years to get to Ephesus. Now that I am here, I am searching for my wife, daughter, and uncle." He gestured toward the grandfather. "I saw this gentleman leaving the synagogue. I thought perhaps he had seen my Uncle Avram at prayer."

The old man shouted, "What is this about Abram? Is he in some kind of trouble again?"

"No, Father. Abram is fine." Turning toward her daughter, Thalia said, "Take your grandfather to the courtyard and keep him company for a while." She waved a hand dismissively as she focused her attention on John Simon again. "Father only catches a word now and then. I have a nephew named Abram, and he obviously thought you were speaking of him. Come and sit and tell me about the people you are searching for." She smiled. "Ephesus is a big city, second only to Rome in population, as you are no doubt aware."

Chapter Twenty-Seven

Channah left the babes sleeping and slipped quietly into the courtyard to bake bread for the household's breakfast. The approaching dawn gave some light ahead of the not-yet-risen sun. Normally, this quiet time was her favorite part of the day. This morning, thinking of the loss of Dorcas, the silence was unsettling.

She stirred the outdoor oven's fire to life and uncovered the loaves that had risen overnight. As she slid the paddle containing the bread into the oven, a noise at the side gate caught her attention. She immediately recognized one of the men who agreed to go to Lydda yesterday, but not the stranger with him.

She hastened to open the gate. "Good morning. Come inside. I have just now put fresh bread into the oven."

The men shuffled wearily into the courtyard. "Good morning," the stranger said. "Where is Dorcas?"

"Alas, sir, Dorcas has passed away."

The man nodded toward his companion. "So Elias told me. I am Peter. I would like to view the body."

Channah's hand flew to cover her mouth. She was astonished that the apostle had come himself instead of sending someone less important to deal with the widows' plea. "Forgive me. We did not expect you so soon."

She wiped her hands. "Thank you for coming. Dorcas's body is laid out in an upper room. Come with me and I will show you."

Channah led the way up the stairs. Widows who had been weeping and praying around the body showed Peter the clothes Dorcas made for them. "We will miss her dreadfully," Anna whimpered.

"I do not know how we will survive without her," Salome agreed. "Thank you for coming. Perhaps you will be able to keep the vultures from—"

Peter held up a hand, and the room fell silent. "Leave us." His eyes were riveted on the corpse, which the women had anointed and wrapped in strips of cloth.

While the others filed out of the room, Channah remembered her bread. She flew down the steps, concerned that the unattended loaves were now burned. In the courtyard, she was relieved to find Elias putting a second paddle of bread into the oven.

"I hope it was all right for me to take the loaves from the oven." Elias wore the shamed face of a wayward boy. "I must confess, I sampled the bread while it was hot."

"You are welcome to the fresh loaves. Thank you for starting the second batch cooking." Channah peered into the oven. "Lydda must be closer than I thought. We thought the earliest you would arrive from there was this evening."

"As soon as we found Peter, he insisted on returning with us right away. We walked all night."

Voices singing a psalm floated on the morning air. Channah turned to locate the source of the sound. It had to be coming from the upper room where Dorcas's body rested. She cocked her head. Something was amiss. The psalm did not have the sedate cadence typical of mourners. As she concentrated on the music, Channah detected a distinctive, high, rich soprano. She knew that voice well. Yet, reason told her it could not be.

"Excuse me," she said to Elias. She ran up the stairs and burst into the upper room from which the singing emanated. Amazingly, Dorcas sat on her bed, singing and helping to unwind long strips of grave wrappings from her leg.

Channah thought she was too stunned to speak. Yet she heard herself shout, “Dorcas! You are alive!”

“Yes. God be praised, I am,” Dorcas replied with a brilliant smile.

Peter sat on the floor in a corner, dozing amid the hubbub of singing, laughing, and crying. The shrill, demanding cry that pierced the air caused his eyes to fly open.

“Oh, my,” Dorcas said. “We have awakened the babies.”

“It is time for them to get up, anyway,” Salome assured her.

When Channah picked up her son and began to dress him, Salome came into the room. Not knowing what else to say, Channah asked, “Will your mistress be concerned about you?”

Salome began to bathe Julia. “I do not plan to leave Dorcas again. When I thought we had lost her, I realized how indebted I am—we all are—to her generosity. I want to remain here and serve her, if she will allow me. And I want to help care for her child.”

Though she marveled at the change in Salome, Channah tried not to show it. “Dorcas will be glad.” She smiled at her friend. “And so am I.”

“Did you know Peter and his wife were staying with a tomb carver in Lydda?”

“No,” Channah replied, uncertain what that bit of trivia had to do with anything.

“He told me that just now. And furthermore, he is going to lodge with a tanner while he remains in Joppa. Tanners are unclean, you know.”

"I am aware that tanners are outcasts." Channah kissed her little boy. "My first husband was a tanner. We were required to live outside Jerusalem's city walls."

"Your *first* husband?" Salome's face broadcast surprise. "But you are so young. I had no idea you have been widowed twice."

"No, only once." Channah said. "I am certain John Simon survived the shipwreck. I cannot explain this, but I know I would feel it if he were no longer alive."

"Of course." There was no conviction in Salome's agreeable response.

As soon as the babies were nursed, Channah and Salome took them to the courtyard. Dorcas was serving bread to Peter and Elias. "Good morning," she called out merrily. "Our guests have been bragging on your baking, Channah."

"Your loaves are the best I have tasted since my last meal prepared by my mother-in-law," Peter declared.

"That is no small compliment," Dorcas said. "I understand she is an accomplished cook."

"Yes, she is."

Channah could feel the heat rising in her face. "I am pleased you are enjoying your meal."

Dorcas came and put an arm on Channah's shoulder. "I must take Peter to the tannery, and drop Elias off at the camp. Will you drive the cart for me?"

"Certainly," Channah murmured, delighted for the opportunity to spend time in the apostle's company.

"This young woman has a gift for dealing with animals," Dorcas said.

"Let me know when you are ready for me to hitch up the cart." Channah put another paddle into the oven. "I made a lot of bread for today. We were expecting a houseful of mourners."

"Perfect," Dorcas said. We will take the extra loaves to the refugee camp."

Chapter Twenty-Eight

Channah was focused too intently on the conversation going on in the cart to pay attention to the fresh morning air. She was not surprised when Elias curled into a ball in the back of the cart and fell asleep.

After Peter answered Dorcas's many questions about the Jerusalem persecution, she thanked him for coming to Joppa.

"I am glad I made the trip," the apostle commented. "I would not want to miss seeing the Lord's miracle of bringing you back to life."

"Surely you have seen such sights before." Dorcas leaned against the side of the cart.

"Yes," Peter agreed, "Jesus raised the dead often when he was here, walking with us in his human body. That was the best time of my life, following Jesus every day, sitting with him each evening, asking questions and enjoying the indescribable pleasure of being in his presence."

Dorcas's smile broke forth again. "I know what you mean."

"I suppose you do." Peter leaned forward. "What was it like?"

"Being dead, you mean? Perhaps I had a vision, or a dream, or maybe it was reality." She did not speak for a long moment before continuing. "I was lying in my bed when most suddenly I was in a different place. I felt great peace wash over me, and I was aware of being loved beyond any measure I have ever known. It seemed I was in that state for only a moment, and then I opened my eyes to find you praying over me."

Channah brought the cart to a stop at the camp.

"Is this the refugee camp?" Peter asked. At Channah's nod, he shook Elias's shoulder. "We have arrived, my son. Are you awake?"

Elias sat erect. "Yes." He leaped from the back of the cart. In no time, his young wife came hurrying as fast as her crippled leg allowed. The couple embraced while the others climbed down from the cart.

"My legs need stretching," Dorcas said. "I must have spent too much time in bed lately." Her lighthearted comment caused everyone to laugh.

"Thank you for bringing the apostle to us," Channah said with a shy glance toward Elias.

"It is I who am indebted," the young man replied. "This has been an awe-inspiring experience." He put an arm around his wife. "Rebecca, you remember Dorcas and Channah."

The young woman nodded a greeting, but looked puzzled.

"But I thought… "

"And meet Peter, an apostle who walked with Jesus throughout his earthly ministry."

"Shalom, Peter." Rebecca turned to her husband. "I understood that Dorcas was…that she…"

Elias smiled. "Peter raised her from the dead."

"No." The apostle spoke gently. "God did the miracle. He graciously permitted me to speak the prayer he chose to answer."

Rebecca's face registered astonishment. She stared at Dorcas, open-mouthed.

Peter visited with refugees while the women distributed food. "He must be exhausted." Dorcas stared toward the apostle kneeling in prayer with a circle of people. She put an arm around Channah's waist. "Thank you for fetching him."

"It was the least I could do." Channah inclined her head to rest on Dorcas's shoulder. "I praise God for your renewed life."

"So do I," Dorcas replied. "I have a child to raise and a grown foster daughter to look after." She tightened her arm around Channah. "There are still many followers of the Way I hope to feed and clothe." She pressed her lips together for a moment before adding softly, "And, God willing, a husband to welcome home."

It was midday before Peter said his goodbyes and climbed into the cart for the trip to the tanner's compound. Channah considered it something of a relief to be away from the two babies for a while. She was attempting to wean them, but it was difficult for her to refuse them breast milk when they cried for it. Today the babes would have no option but to eat the tasty food Salome prepared for them.

"Peter, I know you must be tired," Dorcas said as they rolled up a hill, traveling further away from the city of Joppa. "May I ask one final question before sleep overtakes you?"

"Certainly, my sister."

"Why did the Lord raise me? I mean, why *me*? I am not deserving of his favor."

"No one deserves the grace he heaps on us," Peter replied. "I used to think I would figure him out enough to predict what he would do next, but I was wrong. He told us through the prophet Isaiah that his ways are far above ours." The apostle paused long enough to shift his position in the cart. "I *can* say that he always has a reason for what he does, though it is not always clear to us, and almost never unfolds the way we expect it to. Perhaps you will begin to see his purpose later. On the other hand, he may be working on a grand design you and I will never comprehend this side of Heaven." He yawned. "On this you may depend. His work is aways good."

"Yes," Dorcas agreed. "His way is best."

On the end of another yawn, Peter said, "This trip is an example of how he gets things done so unexpectedly. Elias was getting ready to leave Israel for some unknown destination. Now, he and Rebecca are planning to work with my wife and me for a while to prepare themselves to carry the gospel to other Jews living in exile. This is an answer to prayer for help in my ministry…" His voice trailed away.

"He is asleep," Dorcas murmured.

Familiar unpleasant odors told Channah they were at the tanner's gate. Peter roused when the donkey stopped. He climbed from the cart and said his goodbyes.

"Will you hold meetings in Joppa?" Dorcas asked.

"I am not certain." Peter rubbed his eyes and yawned. "The first order of business is a long nap. Eventually, I must go and get my wife from Lydda." He smiled. "Or perhaps I will send Elias for her. The Lord will show me what to do next."

He turned as if to go, but circled back toward the cart. "Sister Channah, I feel in my spirit I should pray for you. Is there a special burden you bear?"

Channah dropped her eyes when she saw the apostle staring at her. She would never have been bold enough to make a request of him without prompting. "Thank you for asking, sir. I would be most grateful if you would ask the Lord Jesus to reunite me with my family members. We were separated in a shipwreck."

"It will be an honor to intercede on your behalf," Peter said with a weary smile. He waved his hand and disappeared through the tannery gate.

Chapter Twenty-Nine

Dorcas breezed into the courtyard, where Channah and Salome sat watching the children play. “Good afternoon.” She flashed her characteristic smile. “There is a ship docking in the harbor. It appears to be a large vessel. Channah, would you mind driving me down to meet it? It will be easier to use the cart than to carry enough food and clothes for needy people who may be on board.”

“I will be happy to do so.” Channah untied her apron. “The evening bread is baked, and the babies have been fed.”

“Is that all right with you, Salome?” As mistress of the house, Dorcas had every right to give orders. However, she was unfailingly considerate of everyone else’s feelings.

Salome patted Joshua’s dark curls. “I can manage these two.”

Before long, the cart was loaded with fresh bread, nonperishable foodstuffs, and tunics. “What is your number today?” Dorcas asked Channah.

“Um, I will say four.” It was a game they played, seeing which one guessed closest to the number of people to get off the ship needing a tunic. “What is yours?”

“Based on the size of the ship, I will say six.”

“Did you bring that many garments?” Channah asked.

“I brought ten.” Dorcas smiled. “We shall see.”

As soon as they reached the shoreline, a small crowd gathered around the cart. “Are you Dorcas, the clothier?” a young woman holding a baby asked.

“Yes, I am Dorcas.”

Apparently, the young mother was the spokesperson for the group. "We have heard you died and were returned to life by means of a miracle."

"Yes." Dorcas alighted from the cart. "That is true."

"Tell us what happened."

"I will. Here, Channah, grab some tunics and the bread basket." Dorcas turned to face the young woman. "Do you know of the refugee camp outside of town?"

There was a chorus of answers, all affirmative.

"I will be at the camp at sunrise on the first day of the week. Come and hear the whole story." She smiled and turned toward the dock. "If you have the means, bring food for the people of the Way who are staying in the camp."

"It is the same everywhere you go," Channah said.

"Yes." Dorcas glanced back at the crowd milling around the cart. "I was never able to get people to listen when I talked about Jesus before. Now, there is a crowd at the camp every week, and they all get a good dose of the gospel. As Peter said, God's blessings come to us in the most unexpected forms."

"You must be Dorcas," the sailor standing on the dock said.

"Yes, I am."

"The captain said to ask if you are willing to care for a very sick man. Perhaps you can nurse him back to health, but it is more likely he will die."

"I am so sorry," Dorcas said. "I do not take men into my home, only women. My husband is at sea, and it would not be proper."

The sailor shrugged. "The captain thought it was worth asking. He has taken quite a liking to the little girl we picked up with the sick man. Perhaps someone in Caesarea—"

"Little girl?" Channah felt as if she shouted, but the sound that came out of her was closer to a whisper. "What is her name? How old is she?"

"I have no idea." The sailor held his hand out. "She is about this tall."

"May we see her?" Dorcas asked.

The sailor hesitated. "I will ask the captain." He turned and walked away.

Channah was not sure how long her legs would support her. She grasped Dorcas's arm. "It could be Miriam."

"Possibly. Possibly not." Dorcas kept her eyes trained on the ship. "I suppose it would be all right for the man to sleep in the stable while we care for the child."

A one-word scream pierced the air. "Ima!"

Channah dropped the bread basket and ran toward the end of the dock, shouting, "Miriam."

It seemed to take forever for her little girl to reach her. "Oh, Miriam. Praise God." Channah hugged her child close before stepping back to look at her. "You are taller and thinner." She enfolded Miriam in her arms again, kissing her over and over.

"Uncle is sleeping on the ship," Miriam said. "He is very weak."

Channah caught sight of Dorcas leading her donkey onto the dock. "Dorcas and I will take care of him."

"Who is Dorcas?" Miriam asked.

"You will see. Where is your abba?"

The girl's eyes widened. "He is not with you?"

"No." Dread cut a slash across Channah's joy. "We got separated. I thought he was with you and Uncle Avram."

Miriam shook her head. "No."

Channah pulled Miriam closer. "We will find him." She hoped she her words were true.

Dorcas pushed clothes and food aside in the cart. "I spoke with the captain. His men are bringing your uncle ashore. We will nurse him back to health in my son's old bedchamber." She fluffed a blanket over the cart's bed. "That room has been empty far too long."

"You will allow a man in your home? With Captain Joseph at sea?" Channah was pleased, but concerned for Dorcas's reputation.

"I consider you to be part of my family, Channah." Dorcas spoke with finality. "Therefore, your uncle is my relative."

Channah was shocked to see how thin Avram was. Four sailors placed him on the cart, although she thought one man could easily have lifted her uncle's frail body. "Did the people you were with feed you well?" she asked Miriam.

"There were no people, Ima. Uncle and I were by ourselves."

"All this time?"

"Yes. We lived on an island, just the two of us and some wild goats."

Dorcas stopped tucking the blanket around Avram and turned toward Miriam. "What did you eat?"

"We drank goat's milk every morning and evening. Once we found some berries. There were some fig trees with fruit that will be ripe soon, but most days just the milk.

Sometimes uncle did not want too much milk. He always made me drink my portion though."

Channah took a deep breath, trying not to dwell on the privations her daughter and uncle must have suffered while she was safe and comfortable in Dorcas's spacious home. "I made fresh bread this afternoon. Do you want a loaf?"

"Yes, please," the girl replied solemnly. "I will share it with Uncle."

Miriam's eyes bulged when Channah pulled back the cloth covering the basket of food.

"Take what you want for yourself. There will be plenty for Uncle Avram to enjoy when he awakens."

Chapter Thirty

When Channah shook Avram's shoulder, the old man groaned. "Channah," he whispered. "God be praised. I feared I would never see your sweet face again." He coughed. "How is John Simon?"

"He is not here," she replied. "Have some broth. You are as thin as a reed."

Avram sipped at the cup she held to his lips. "Ah. I have never tasted anything so wonderful."

"Dorcas told me to start slow. If you can tolerate soup, we will add bread and then cheese tomorrow."

"Who is Dorcas?" Avram asked between gulps of broth.

"She is a wonderfully kind believer in Jesus. She took me in after the shipwreck. I do not know how I could have survived without her help." Channah poured a half cup of wine and handed it to her uncle. "This is her house."

"What did you mean when you said John Simon is not here? Where is he?"

"I do not know, Uncle. I have not seen him since the day of our shipwreck. All this time I assumed he was with you and Miriam."

"Lost at sea," Avram murmured. "May God have mercy on his soul."

"Many people have tried to convince me he is dead." Channah smoothed hair away from her uncle's forehead. "They also told me I would never see you or Miriam again."

Avram drank more soup. "It is a miracle that the child and I survived on that island."

"But here you are. Since God has brought you back to me, perhaps he will see fit to do another such work and reunite us with John Simon."

The old man set his cup aside, relaxed onto the bed, and closed his eyes. "We will pray."

"Speaking of miracles, I have something to show you." Channah rose and moved toward the doorway.

"Perhaps after I sleep."

"As you wish. After your nap, I will bring my little boy to meet you. If I can pry him loose from Miriam, that is."

Avram's eyes flew open. He propped himself up on one elbow. "Your…you mean to say you have a *son*?"

"Yes, Uncle. He is the reason I was so nauseous on our sea voyage. I named him Joshua."

"Joshua. That is a good name. A son. Praise God from whom all blessings flow."

Channah found Joshua taking his afternoon nap in Miriam's arms. She took him to Avram's bed chamber, only to discover her uncle had also fallen asleep. She smiled and nestled Joshua close by the old man. "Rest well, beloved twosome." she whispered.

When Channah rejoined the other women in the courtyard, Miriam ran to her, and the two hugged as if they had been parted for years instead of a few brief moments.

"What do you think of your little brother?" Salome asked, as she sat mending a tunic.

"He is the sweetest, cutest, smartest baby ever." Miriam's face glowed with a broad smile. "He looks exactly like Abba."

Channah laughed. "I happen to agree with you. I believe Uncle Avram will make three of us who feel that way."

"I want to feed him and dress him and take care of him all the time."

"You can help with those things." Channah clasped her daughter to her. "First, you and Uncle must regain your strength."

"Uncle likes to sleep all day, but I am strong." Miriam held up her skinny arms as evidence. "May I hold the girl baby now?"

Channah cast her eyes toward Dorcas. "If you approve."

"Of course." Dorcas smiled. "It is time for her nap. So, she may be fussy."

Miriam sat on a stone bench and cuddled Julia.

Salome turned to Channah. "How is your uncle?"

"He is very weak. I am hoping he will get better with plenty of rest and good food." After settling on a bench next to Miriam, Channah opened a work bag and took out her spinning.

"Uncle loves Ima's bread," Miriam volunteered. "He spoke of it often on the island where we stayed. He does not care for goat's milk, but that is all we had most days."

Channah kept her spindle moving, stealing a glance at her daughter. "Uncle has always been fond of goat's milk. He actually prefers it."

"Not anymore." Miriam shook her head. "Some days he drank almost nothing."

Channah fought to keep the tears that formed from spilling onto her cheeks. She realized what her child did not—that Avram had denied himself nourishment to make sure Miriam had enough. It was no mystery why he was so emaciated.

Dorcas broke the awkward silence. "Miriam, did I hear you say you were on an island where no one lives? If there was no harbor, how did you make your way to the ship that brought you back to Joppa?"

"Uncle said we should build a fire the sailors could see and maybe come to the island to see what was happening. We spent many hours dragging dried branches to the top of a hill for kindling." Miriam rocked back and forth as she spoke, lulling Julia to sleep. "When I saw a ship in the distance, we took a torch up the hill to set the wood afire."

"And so your uncle's plan worked," Dorcas commented.

Miriam kept her eyes on the babe in her arms. "No. We were never able to get a good blaze going before the ships sailed on by. Three times we had to start over. Then, one night, there was a big noise. Uncle said it must have been a lightning strike. It set our wood pile on fire. By sunrise, the big ship had come. Some men came in a little rowboat and took us to it."

"Now that Julia has gone to sleep, I'll put her in her cradle." Salome stood and took the baby from Miriam. "Your story is truly amazing. Perhaps your uncle will speak at the weekly worship gathering. After we hear from the Apostle Peter, that is."

Dorcas pressed her lips together for a moment before saying, "Miriam, perhaps you would like to go with Salome and help her put Julia to bed."

As soon as the door closed behind Salome, Dorcas spoke. "Peter has left Joppa."

"So soon?" Bethel stopped carding wool for a long moment.

"He was concerned for his wife's safety." Dorcas sighed. "Persecution against the Way has broken out in Lydda."

Although she continued to spin, Channah's thoughts turned toward her family. Just as John Simon predicted, oppression was spreading beyond Jerusalem. She saw God's hand in delaying her travel plans because she needed Dorcas's shelter during her pregnancy and the birth of her son. Then, even though she did not know it, she had to wait in Joppa until her uncle and daughter were rescued from the unnamed island. Now, as soon as Avram was strong enough to travel, she felt it was the right time to take her family to a safer place.

If only John Simon had been with her uncle and Miriam. Where in the big, wide world was he? Stranded on some unknown shore, naked and starving? But John Simon was resourceful. Her husband was strong. He would fight to survive. Someday, somehow, he would come home to her, God willing.

Chapter Thirty-One

Thalia led John Simon into a small, cluttered room. "What is your wife's name?" she asked.

"Channah. She is with her Uncle Avram and our daughter Miriam."

"All common names," Thalia muttered as she took one of several small wooden boxes from her shelf. "I do not recall such a family, but my memory is not always reliable. That is why I write things down. How long ago did she arrive in Ephesus?"

"That I do not know, possibly as much as two years ago. We were separated in a shipwreck."

Thalia opened the box and took out a stack of loose papyrus sheets. "Hmm, here is a Channah. She came to Ephesus six months ago with her father, Perez. No, too young, fourteen and never married. She is not the one." "She continued poring over the parchments. "Avram, thirty and willing to be married to a wealthy woman of any age."

"Not this year," Thalia mumbled, as she took a second box from the shelf.

In the silence broken only by the sound of dry pages moving against each other, John Simon asked, "I have no reason to believe Channah is seeking a husband."

Thalia chuckled. "Young man, I keep track of *all* local Jews, whether they come to me to arrange a marriage or not. I have better records than the Roman census." She glanced at him and smiled. "Someone who is happily married today may be in the market tomorrow. For example, a man's wife dies. I check my files and see the deceased woman had children who must be cared for. So, I go to mourn the poor widower's loss and at the same time offer him an immediate selection of brides.

Complete, accurate information on demand is good business, you see."

"Do your records show who follows the Way?"

Thalia's eyes flicked from the page in her hands to John Simon's face, and back again. "Do you mean the crazy people who claim the Messiah has come but was crucified?"

"I refer to the followers of Jesus."

"I know a man who insists on that story. According to my father, the rabbi considered banning him from the synagogue. After a lot of discussion, he decided to let him stay." She rolled her eyes. "He went to Jerusalem for Passover and Pentecost four years ago. There must have been something in the water. He has never been the same." She sighed. "He has asked me to find him a bride, but I doubt any family will be willing to give him their daughter. He has a bad eye, and now he has become irrationally dedicated to the Way."

"So, you do not keep account of the Jews who follow the Way?"

"I never said that." Thalia eyed him again. "Blasphemers want to get married like everyone else. I offer my services to anyone who is willing to pay my price. It is just that some cases are more difficult."

"Where can I find this one-eyed believer you spoke of?"

The matchmaker placed her hands in front of her, and then rubbed the fingers of her right hand across her open left palm. "You have no idea how expensive writing materials have become."

John Simon took a coin and deposited it in her hand.

Thalia examined the coin before tucking it inside her ample bosom. "Are you a follower of the Way?"

"Yes, I am."

"Alexander lives just down the street, nine houses to your left from my front door. He is not home, however. He operates a ferry on the river Cayster, rowing tradesmen to and from the opposite shore for a fee. I will give you directions.

"Thank you." John Simon stood. "My wife's uncle will certainly connect with other followers of the Way. I will seek out Alexander and find out what he knows."

"Before you go." Thalia gestured for him to sit. "Suppose you do not find your wife among the people of the Way. What will you do?"

"I will continue my search. I have been totally focused on getting to Ephesus, hoping Channah would be here waiting for me. I have not given much thought to other possibilities."

The matchmaker dipped her pen and wrote on a scrap of papyrus. "John Simon, from—Joppa?"

"Originally Ephesus. Lately from Bethlehem."

"Bethlehem, then. Wife and other relatives lost at sea. Not yet ready to consider marriage as of this date." She appeared to be writing down the words as she spoke them. "You should settle down in Ephesus, get married, and wait for your family to come and find you." She shrugged. "If they do, you have two wives. If they never come, you have not wasted your life in a hopeless venture."

"No." John Simon said. "I will never have any wife other than Channah." He hugged himself and rubbed his hands up and down his arms. "I cannot sit still and wait, fearing the whole time Channah is struggling to get here. That is simply not in my nature. I am a man of action."

"What a pity. This Channah of yours, she must be a very special lady."

"She is to me." John Simon stood. At the doorway, he turned to face Thalia. "As you said, Jesus was crucified. After he died, they sealed him into a tomb. Three days later, he took up his life again. He is our Messiah."

"If you and Alexander want to think someone died and came back to life, fine. That is none of my concern."

"It is not a matter of thinking. I know." John Simon could not prevent himself from smiling. "I heard Jesus preach, and I believed what he said long before he was crucified. Then I saw him later, alive and well, after he arose. It was him."

"That is impossible," Thalia said, with a dismissive wave of her hand.

"Yes, it is. That is the point, is it not? Human beings do what is possible. God does what is not. You and the leader of your synagogue would do well to pay attention to what Alexander has to say. Shalom."

Chapter Thirty-Two

John Simon followed a well-worn path to Alexander's crossing. He expected to find a platform raft. Instead, the ferry was a rowboat. He assumed the muscular young man operating the oars was Alexander. The patch he wore over his left eye confirmed his identity.

A passenger leapt onto the river bank as soon as the boat was close to the stone landing. He and Alexander lifted a sled stacked with baskets ashore. The man grabbed the rope handle of his sled and hurried away, dragging his load of baskets behind.

"Good morning, friend," Alexander said. "Do you wish to go to the other side?"

"Thank you, no," John Simon replied. "I am looking for Alexander."

"That is me." Alexander rested his arms on the oars, but did not leave his boat. "What brings you here, if not to cross the river?"

"My name is John Simon. I am looking for my family. Thalia the matchmaker told me you are a follower of the Way. Do you know of a woman named Channah? She would have come to Ephesus with our daughter, Miriam, and her Uncle Avram."

Alexander's smile proclaimed his belief as emphatically as his words. "I have not seen the people you describe. However, I do follow Jesus of Nazareth, and have ever since the day of Pentecost four years back. Shall I tell you about my trip to Jerusalem, and the marvels I witnessed there?"

"I would love to hear your story." John Simon stepped nearer the boat and squatted to put his eyes level with Alexander's. "And if you like, I will share what I know of Jesus. I heard him preach--."

“What?” Alexander interrupted. “You actually heard words fall from the Master’s own lips?” He maneuvered his rowboat snug against the stones of the bank. “I must return to the other side. People are crossing to go into town this time of the day, and I cannot disappoint my regular customers. Please ride with me so we can talk.”

John Simon hesitated. “It will be harder for you to row with an extra passenger.”

“What does it matter if my arms get tired while my heart is being filled?” Alexander put his hands on the oars and beckoned with his head. “Come aboard, please.”

With no further discussion, John Simon stepped into the rowboat. He sat on the wooden plank bench nearest Alexander, facing him. “I see you have an extra pair of oars. I will help you row.”

“As a young ferryman, I lost my oars one day and had to paddle to the shore with my hands. Since then, I always carry spares.”

John Simon pulled a pair of smoothly-hewn oars from beneath the wooden benches. He dug deeply into the dark water, matching Alexander’s strokes one-for-one.

‘You are no novice, I see,” Alexander commented.

“I have been mostly at sea for more than two years,” John Simon replied. “Not by choice, however. I still think of myself as a shepherd.”

“Are you a slave?”

“No. My family and I were on our way to Ephesus when we were shipwrecked. Then, a centurion I saved from drowning compelled me to go to all the way to Rome with him.”

Alexander nodded. “I would like to hear about your adventures someday. But first, tell me about Jesus.”

"I was bitter toward my father, and my anger eventually expanded to include all Romans," John Simon said. "I joined the zealots, determined to kill as many Romans as I could before they took my life. One day, when I was being pursued by a soldier, it seemed to be a good time to disappear into a crowd. I ended up sitting on a mountainside, listening to Jesus teach. The place where he told us to sit down was a natural amphitheater. Amazingly, even from some distance, I could hear every word clearly."

When John Simon stopped to collect his thoughts, Alexander said, "Please, tell me everything you remember. Every single word. Stop rowing if you wish. Just speak."

"He started out by saying, 'Blessed are the poor in spirit, because the kingdom of God is theirs.'"

All day long, John Simon and Alexander crisscrossed the river, praising God, singing psalms, and sharing remembrances. A few passengers joined in the conversation, asking questions about Jesus and the Kingdom of God. One fellow called them madmen. Most ignored them.

As sundown approached, John Simon helped Alexander drag his boat to a storage shed. "I pay the farmer to lock my boat in his barn at night," Alexander said as he closed the shed door behind him. "Otherwise, thieves would put me out of business." He smiled and clapped John Simon's shoulder. "Speaking of business, are you interested in being my partner?" He opened his coin pouch. "Together we rowed across the river faster, carried more passengers, and made more money than usual. I will split today's earnings with you."

John Simon held up a hand. "There is no need to share your coins with me. It has been a long time since I enjoyed anything more than today's conversations." He hitched his belt. "I thank you for the business proposition, but tomorrow I am going to strike out for Israel. Since Channah is not here in Ephesus, then she must be on her way, probably by land. I doubt she has the means to earn passage on another ship."

"Do you not think it would be wise to wait here for your wife to catch up with you?"

John Simon shrugged. "I will never have peace sitting still. I could not sleep at night, worrying that she was somewhere on the road, trying to make her way here with a child and an old man to care for."

"I understand." Alexander nodded. "If I had a wife, no doubt I would do the same thing. You do realize what a dangerous and difficult journey you are undertaking?"

"Perhaps it is just as well that I do not. I will press on in the same way I have been, trying to make progress every day without considering the difficulties of the morrow."

"I have a cousin in Laodicea. If you—I mean to say *when*—you get that far, he will extend hospitality to you. Tonight, you must lodge at my house. My mother and father will be so excited to hear about the sermon you spoke of. They will pack food for you, for tomorrow's journey."

The next morning, John Simon's last stop on his way out of Ephesus was at the matchmaker's house.

Thalia peered at him through her cracked door. Then she smiled broadly and flung the door open wide. "You changed your mind about taking another wife. I knew you would, but not so soon."

"No, I will never take another wife," John Simon replied. "But I do want to transact some business with you."

Thalia crossed her arms and stared at him for a moment. Finally, she beckoned him inside with a self-satisfied smirk. “I know of a woman who is not fussy about the formality of marriage. Come back to my office.”

John Simon settled into a chair. “I am leaving for Israel, in the hope of meeting Channah somewhere between here and Jerusalem.”

“So, if your family comes to Ephesus, they will find you have come and gone. What a brilliant plan.”

Ignoring Thalia’s sarcasm, he continued speaking. “Yesterday you claimed to know or know of everyone in the local Jewish community.”

Her smile broadened. “I do.”

“Then let me make you an offer. When Channah and her uncle and our daughter get to Ephesus, send them to Alexander.”

Thalia shook her head, “I hardly think—”

John Simon interrupted, “And I will pay you twice what you would charge to find me a new wife.”

“Twice?”

“You heard right.”

“How do I know you will pay?”

“I have already left the money with Alexander, along with instructions for him to settle my debt when you bring Channah to him.” In response to her skeptical frown, he added, “What do you have to lose? You did say that you keep track of everyone, whether they seek a spouse or not.” John Simon did not mention that he also left money for Channah with Alexander. He saw no reason for Thalia to have that information.

“I will prepare a contract.”

The matchmaker cut a rectangle from a roll of papyrus and began writing. When she finished, John

Simon read over the document. “Agreed.” He took the reed pen she offered and signed his name.

Thalia took the papyrus and re-read the words she herself had written. “So, all I have to do is let Alexander know where to locate your Channah when, and if, she arrives in Ephesus?”

“And Miriam, and Avram.”

“Fine.” Thalia placed the signed document into one of her numerous wooden boxes. “What makes you think you can trust Alexander? He could already be at the marketplace, spending your coins on amphoras of wine.”

“I passed the whole day with him yesterday. I am convinced he is honest.” John Simon picked up his knapsack. “I will be going now. Thank you.”

Thalia followed him to the door. “Suppose your family makes it to Ephesus. Do you not understand that your wife will be found but then you will be lost?” She shook her head. “The notion is hopeless.”

“There is always hope with the Lord, Thalia,” John Simon replied.

As he exited her house, she called after him, “I wish you luck, even if you are as unhinged as all the other followers of the Way I know. You are nice people, but crazy.”

Chapter Thirty-Three

Shortly before sunrise, Dorcas stepped into her courtyard, where Channah already had bread in the outdoor oven.

"Good morning. There is nothing so delightful as the smell of baking bread." Dorcas yawned and stretched her arms. "I thank God every time I awaken to a new day of life."

"Good morning." Channah turned and smiled. She set aside a paddle filled with fresh loaves and slid another batch in to cook.

"Where is your uncle?" Dorcas asked, as she selected two small loaves and sat on a stone bench. "He is normally the first to sample your bread each morning."

"He is on his way into town." Channah dusted her hands on her apron. "He is hoping to find work as a shepherd."

"But he is not strong enough yet to work."

"He is still weak," Channah admitted. "Nevertheless, he feels he must earn some wages." She came and sat next to her friend.

"I hoped Joseph would be home by now." Dorcas kept her eyes down, and picked at the hem of her tunic. Then she took a deep breath. "If he has not yet arrived in the Spring when the ships begin to sail, I have decided to pay your family's passage to Ephesus."

"You have done so much for us, providing a place to live, and food, and clothing. Not to mention nursing Uncle back to health and taking care of me when I was pregnant. We must not impose on you any longer."

"You are no imposition." Dorcas patted Channah's hand. "You have helped me with my sheep and taught the women how to process wool. I would be more than pleased to have you and your family stay with me permanently." Dorcas tucked her top lip underneath the bottom one. "No one understands better than I that you must go and try to find your husband." After a moment, she added, "And if things are not to your liking in Ephesus, you will always have a home here in Joppa, with Joseph and me."

"You are too kind." Channah could not stop the tears from spilling onto her cheeks. "I have no words to tell you how grateful I am for all you have done."

Brushing away her own tears, Dorcas hugged Channah. Then she stood. "We shall begin preparations." She smiled. "You must finish weaning Julia. So much to do." Dorcas strode away without a backward glance.

Channah continued baking, realizing the journey she longed to make was almost at hand. She prayed while she worked, as she did every morning, that John Simon was alive and well. She resolved not to be fearful, nor to listen to the well-meaning women who predicted she would never see her husband again. God raised Dorcas from the dead and brought Miriam and Avram home. She had no doubt he was all powerful. On the other hand, James was beheaded and the faithful apostle Peter was in hiding. As John Simon often said, the Lord moved in mysterious ways to accomplish his purposes. She cast her eyes toward the sky, praying God's plans included making her family whole again. Whatever happened, she now had Avram, Miriam, and Joshua. Each one was a treasure, for which she vowed never to stop being thankful. Dorcas had showered immeasurable kindness on her. *Am I wrong to ask for more?*

The cry of a baby told Channah it was time to dress and feed the children. She smiled and whispered as she went into the house, "Thank you again, Father, for giving me John Simon's son."

Every time she looked into Joshua's eyes, as she did this morning, she saw her husband's large, luminous brown eyes looking back at her. No sooner had she and Salome taken the babies to the courtyard than the stable boy let Avram in the side gate.

Channah offered her uncle fresh bread. “I was not expecting you to return until evening.”

Avram held a loaf in his hands and turned it round and round. “I heard some disturbing news in town.”

Salome and Channah exchanged glances, waiting for the old man to continue.

“There was an incident yesterday. Ruffians tore up the refugee camp and beat up everyone they could catch. They warned them to turn from the Way.” He swallowed a bite of bread. “This is a bad turn of events.”

“Who were the attackers?” Salome asked the question that was also in Channah’s mind.

“Who knows?” Avram shrugged. “I came back to warn Dorcas. Then I will go to the camp and offer whatever assistance I can to the people there.”

Salome stood abruptly. “Dorcas must know immediately.”

Soon everyone poured from the house into the courtyard, all talking at once. Dorcas motioned for quiet. “Salome tells me you have news, Avram,” she said.

Channah turned toward Miriam. “Take your little brother inside and give him a date cake.”

Miriam took Joshua’s hand but did not move. “May I not hear what Uncle has to say?”

“Your little girl did a lot of growing up on the island. You cannot protect her from the evil in the world by keeping her ignorant. She deserves to know the situation,” Avram said gently.

“All right,” Channah murmured.

"There was much talk in the marketplace this morning about a raid on the refugee camp last night," Avram said. "I do not know what is true or false, but it is clear something happened. I am on my way to see for myself. Meanwhile, it is a good idea to be alert."

Dorcas spoke up. "I will go with you to the camp. I was preparing to take food out there anyway." She nodded toward the animal shelter. "We can take the cart. Salome, close the public entrance to the business." She smiled. "There is no need for concern. You know how rumors fly around. We will know more after Avram and I visit the camp."

"Shall I drive you?" Channah asked after the women filed out of the courtyard.

"No." The calmness Dorcas displayed earlier was replaced by a look of concern. "Stay here with your children."

Avram sank onto a stone bench. "I should go alone. If what I heard is true, the road may not be safe. You could be a particular target, Dorcas."

"I? A target? I am well known in Joppa."

"Yes," Avram agreed. "Perhaps too well-known, and not only for your charity. Enemies of the Way do not want people to hear your testimony."

A heavy silence settled over the small group, as the truth of Avram's words sank in. Finally, Dorcas addressed him. "You are very wise, but I must go with you. Do you have a dagger?"

"Yes, indeed," Avram replied. "It was very useful on the island."

"Perhaps you should bring it." Dorcas rose and smiled brightly. "Let us remember the admonition throughout the holy scriptures to be strong and courageous. If you will harness the donkey, Avram, I will gather provisions for the refugees."

Channah retied her apron. "Let me help you."

Chapter Thirty-Four

The babies were sleeping, but no one else wanted to go to bed until Dorcas returned from the camp. The women sat in the courtyard, spinning or carding fibers. Even the stable boy crouched silently by the gate.

"It is getting dark," Bethel declared.

There were grunts acknowledging the obvious, but no one offered an additional comment. After punching down her dough, Channah formed the next day's bread into fist-sized portions. The loaves would rise during the night and be ready to bake at sunrise, as usual.

The bray of Dorcas's donkey announced Dorcas and Avram's arrival. The stable boy leapt to open the gate. Channah stopped her embroidery, straining to see faces in the dimming light. Fatigue was all she could discern.

After a moment of total silence, the women in the courtyard all spoke at once.

"What happened?"

"Are things as bad as we heard?"

"Was anyone hurt?"

Dorcas accepted Avram's help climbing from the cart. "Patience." She held up a restraining hand. "As soon as I catch my breath, I will tell you what we found out."

The stable boy tugged at the donkey's harness to urge her along. Avram tapped the boy on the shoulder and motioned toward where the women sat in a semi-circle. "I will attend to the animal."

The lad glanced toward Dorcas. When she gave him a slight nod, he leaned against the house wall, behind the women.

"Some men went to the refugee camp before dawn this morning," Dorcas began. "There were about a dozen of them. They destroyed the first tent they came to and beat everyone inside."

"Everyone?" Salome questioned. "Not just the men?"

"A husband and wife, and their five children," Dorcas replied. When a buzz rippled through the gathered women, she spread her hands and waved for quiet. "The rest of the refugees came running to help. As soon as the thugs realized they were outnumbered, they ran away. It could have been much worse than it was."

Bethel's voice had a tremor in it when she asked, "Are we in danger?"

"Violence against followers of Jesus has become common in Jerusalem. I hope this was a random incident here in Joppa. However, I think it would be wise for you to go about the city in groups for a while, until things settle down."

"Was Saul of Tarsus among the attackers?" Salome asked.

"No one knows who they were." Dorcas put a hand to her head and sighed. "I doubt Saul was involved. He would have arrived with armed men and arrest orders. For all we know, the camp's attackers were common thieves who thought they found a ripe opportunity."

Avram emerged from the animal shelter. He went to the spot where the stable boy stood and squatted beside him.

"In a moment," Dorcas said, "I will ask Avram to quote from the holy writings. Then we will pray. After that, I suggest we all get a good night's sleep."

After Avram's recitation and prayer, the women filed silently from the courtyard. Dorcas caught Channah's hand and whispered, "Wait."

Soon only Dorcas, Avram, and Channah remained.

"I know it is late," Dorcas glanced toward Avram, then looked at Channah. "Your uncle and I had a serious discussion on the way home from the camp." She paused, seeming to struggle to find words.

Finally, Avram spoke up. "We believe the time has come for our journey to Ephesus to continue."

"Are you strong enough, Uncle?" Channah asked.

"I am as strong as I ever again expect to be."

Although Channah doubted Avram's full recovery from his ordeal on the island, she accepted his opinion. She stared down at her folded hands. Questions crowded into her mind, but she could not immediately sort them out.

"I do not know when my Joseph will come home," Dorcas admitted. Then she added softly, "Or if he ever will. Such is the life of a sailor's wife." She drew a deep breath. "If you agree, I will arrange your passage on the next local merchant vessel that comes into the harbor headed north. They are slow, because they make many stops. They are safer than the big ships, however, because they hug the coastline all the way."

Channah remembered the last words of the Psalm Avram quoted earlier. *Be of good courage, and he shall strengthen your heart, all ye that hope in the Lord.* "When shall we go?"

"How soon can you be ready?" Dorcas asked.

"We have few possessions," Channah answered. "Only our clothing."

"I have already set aside many things to send with you." Dorcas nodded. "You will have the tools and supplies you need to set up a weaving business. Plus, blankets, new clothes, sleeping mats, and a small tent for shelter."

"But, Dorcas," Channah protested. "You have already done far too much for me. You must not—"

"Nonsense. It has been a joy to have you here. You have worked hard and never asked for wages. Furthermore, the women and I agree you make the best bread in Joppa. This is the least I can do for you and your family."

"Thank you." Channah brushed away her tears. "As much as I want to get to Ephesus, it is hard to leave you when things are in turmoil here."

"There is always trouble of some kind. Painful as it is, I knew someday you would have to go away. And now the time has come." She leaned and kissed Channah's cheek. "What I did not know is that I would have to give up Julia."

"The baby? Give her up?" From the corner of her eye, Channah saw Avram's nod.

"Do you remember Elias and Rebecca? Peter has commissioned them to witness to the Jews in Smyrna. They will be on the ship with you." Dorcas tilted her head back and closed her eyes. "They have agreed to take Julia with them, and raise her as their own child."

"But why?" Channah was stunned, knowing how dearly Dorcas loved the baby she was giving away.

"The man whose family was beaten told us the attackers kept asking him where to find the foreign child Dorcas is hiding," Avram said.

She shuddered as she put her hand on Dorcas's shoulder. "They actually spoke your name?"

"Yes," Avram said. "Everyone around Joppa has heard of the miracle of this woman's raising, and the religious leaders are angry about it. They will use any excuse to silence her."

"I refuse to be intimidated." Dorcas's voice was strong. "However, I will be more cautious. Some young men from the camp will come tomorrow, to keep the women safe while I make more permanent arrangements for a household guard." She took Channah's hand and squeezed it. "More than anything, we must protect the children. That is why you and Avram need to take Joshua and Miriam away now." Dorcas brushed away a tear. "And why, with a heavy heart, I have to let go of my precious little Julia."

Chapter Thirty-Five

Two days later Channah led her family down the steep footpath to the harbor. She carried Julia, making sure Miriam was between herself and Avram. Joshua rode on his great uncle's back, which he seemed to think was a grand lark. Dorcas, Elias, and Rebecca met them by the sea at dawn, along with a burly cart driver Channah took to be Dorcas's new bodyguard.

Avram stood Joshua next to Channah. "Stay here with your ima," he instructed the boy. "I will help Elias load our belongings."

"Thank you, Dorcas." Channah fought back tears. "I have no words strong enough to thank you for all you have done for us."

Dorcas shook her head. "Please. If I start crying, I may never be able to stop. We will see each other again. If not in this life, then in the next." She drew in her breath and stood ramrod straight. "Help Julia get acquainted with Rebecca as quickly as you can."

When Rebecca held out her arms, the baby leaned toward them. Channah shifted the baby into Rebecca's waiting embrace.

"Hello, little darling. I have been hoping for a child to love. Elias and I will do our best to be a good abba and ima to you." Glancing toward Dorcas, Rebecca said, "She is beautiful."

"Yes," Dorcas agreed. "She is."

"My ima take me on a boat," Joshua informed everyone.

"Really?" Rebecca smiled down on him, still cuddling Julia close. "What a grown-up boy you must be."

"We find my abba."

Channah tousled the top of her little son's head. "That is our prayer."

When Avram and Elias joined the women, Channah knew they could tarry no longer. She hugged Dorcas one last time. "I will pray every day for Captain Joseph's safe return. God be with you, my sister."

"And I will pray for you to be safe and to find your husband," Dorcas whispered into Channah's ear. "Take good care of the children. I love all of you dearly."

Channah picked up Joshua and turned toward the ship. Julia began to wail when Rebecca carried her away from Dorcas.

The last sight Channah had of Dorcas, she was leaning against her donkey, sobbing her heart out.

As soon as they claimed their spot on the deck, Channah took Julia and tried to comfort her. When the baby continued to weep, she said, "There is one solution that always works. I will let her have my milk." With Rebecca's help, she moved the sleeping mats to create as private a niche as possible. Sure enough, Julia quieted and nursed.

When Joshua realized what was happening, he climbed into Channah's lap and cried for his mother's milk. "No, Joshua," Channah admonished him. "You are too old to suck. She laughed to see his protruding bottom lip, which only served to make him cry louder.

Avram peeked over the sleeping mat barrier. "What is wrong with the boy? Is he hurt?"

"No," Channah replied. "He wants to remain a baby."

"Not baby," Joshua protested.

"Come with me Joshua," Avram boomed. "I want to show you something."

"What?" the boy asked between whimpers.

"It is a surprise. You must come and see."

Channah was grateful for her uncle's intervention, and surprised that Joshua responded by toddling toward the sound of Avram's beckoning voice.

Soon the ship began to move away from the harbor. Channah handed the sleeping Julia over to her new mother. "I will unroll one of the mats for her to nap on."

"Never mind," Rebecca said. "Maybe if I hold her while she sleeps, she will start getting used to me."

"Possibly." Channah went in search of Joshua. She found him sitting the low wall of the deck, laughing, with his feet dangling over the side of the ship. She shivered, despite Avram's tight hold the boy. How fearless he is, she thought. *Just like his father.* Despite her best efforts, she could not stop reliving the shipwreck. *Lord Jesus, please keep us safe.*

Channah was beginning to feel queasy when the sailors tossed the anchor overboard. Dorcas had warned the ship's progress would be slow. Still, the first port of call came sooner than expected.

"What is happening?" Rebecca asked. "Why are we stopping?"

"Perhaps the men know." Channah remained still on her sleeping mat. The nausea was much milder than on the previous voyage. Still, she did not feel like risking the contents of her stomach by standing. After Rebecca took Julia and wandered away, she nibbled on one of the ginger-flavored drops Dorcas had sent with her. The ship was no longer moving forward, but even at anchor it bobbed up and down in the restless sea water.

Channah realized she must have dozed off for a while when she felt the ship begin to move forward again.

Rebecca was back in their designated space. She played with Julia, clapping the baby's hands together with hers and making funny faces.

"Ah, you are awake," Rebecca observed. "We stopped to let a passenger get off the boat. They took him ashore in a rowboat. Elias said that is because there is no harbor here. So, this is as close to land as the ship can get."

"I wonder how many such stops we must make," Channah murmured. "I am sorry to be such dull company. Dorcas told me the seasickness will pass in two or three days."

"I have a touch of dizziness myself," Rebecca admitted. "The men and the children do not seem to be affected. Elias said Apolonia is our next stop. He asked one of the sailors. Have you been there?"

"No." Channah closed her eyes. She was grateful Avram and Miriam were looking after Joshua. For herself, she longed only to return to the oblivion of sleep.

The next day, Channah was miserable. After that, she grew more accustomed to the ship's movement each day. By the time the ship anchored at Caesarea, Channah was able to cope with the ship's constant movement without feeling ill. At night, she awoke at the slightest noise, always aware of the possibility of another shipwreck. She battled her fears with prayer.

At Acco, the ship was at anchor long enough for the men to go ashore. Avram brought back fresh loaves of bread, oranges, and a skin of wine. Channah allowed herself the luxury of a dampened rag to wash herself and the children with a small amount of fresh water. She felt marginally cleaner afterward, hoping never to have another gritty sea-water bath after the end of the voyage.

“Would you like to try one of these?” Rebecca held out meat wrapped in what appeared to be fresh flatbread. “Elias and I think they are delicious.”

The food was most appealing to the eye. However, Channah knew Rebeca and Elias had nothing but a gift of coins from Dorcas to live on. “I must decline. I filled myself on apricots and bread. Do you care for some fruit?”

“Thank you, but no. I have just finished two of these.” She put a rag around the meat and bread concoction. “I will save this one for later.”

Chapter Thirty-Six

Elias fell ill the next evening. “Perhaps it is something he ate,” Rebecca explained. “No doubt he will be better tomorrow.”

Rebecca’s low moan awoke Channah soon after dark. By morning, both Elias and Rebecca were feverish.

Avram, Channah, and Miriam alternated caring for the sick and keeping the babies busy away from them. At their next stop, the ship took on a foul-smelling cargo. “Those small amphoras stink of rotting flesh,” Channah told Avram.

“That makes sense,” Avram agreed. “A sailor told me they contain purple dye. It is made from the snails, presumably dead ones, that inhabit these waters. I understand it is quite expensive, and the Romans are very fond of clothing colored with it.”

“The stench would make a well person sick.” She swapped Julia from her right to her left arm. “It is surely not good for Rebecca and Elias.”

“I notice they have lost all interest in food,” Avram observed. “What little they eat does not stay with them.”

“Thank God we are still some distance from Ephesus. Surely, they will recover before we arrive there.”

“Go round again, Uncle,” Joshua begged from his piggy-back position on Avram’s back.

“Uncle is too tired.” Channah motioned to him. “Come with me while I nurse Julia.

As Avram sat the boy down, Joshua asked, “Me, too?”

“All right.” In response to Avram’s raised eyebrow, she said, “I know I should wean both of them, but it is just too much effort right now.”

Avram put an arm on her shoulder. “You must rest, little one.”

“You have not called me that in years.” Channah inclined her head against his chest. “You are the one who needs rest. You should lie down while I feed the children.”

“Perhaps I will take a nap.” Avram wrinkled his nose. “As far away from that wretched purple dye as I can get.”

The next day the ship’s captain came and stood beside the ailing couple. “What is the trouble with your companions?”

“They fell ill just this side of Acco,” Avram answered.

The captain bent and put the back of his hand on Elias’s forehead. “As I suspected. He burns.”

Channah dipped a rag in wine and applied it to Rebecca’s face. “We are doing our best to calm the fever.”

Straightening, the captain spoke sternly. “Sometime tomorrow we will arrive in Seleucia Pieria. If these people are not up and about by then, I will put them off my ship.”

“No,” Channah whispered.

Avram stood and faced the captain. “But why? Their passage has been paid all the way to Smyrna.”

“It is bad luck for someone to die on board. It brings down a permanent curse on the vessel.” He glanced toward Elias. “They will not survive to Smyrna. Look how pale he is. She as well. I simply cannot risk having the crew abandon the ship because of the goddess Fortuna’s disfavor.”

Rebecca appeared to attempt to speak, but her words were too slurred to be understood. Elias did not move or open his eyes.

Without further comment, the captain turned on his heel and left the area.

Channah was about to speak when her uncle asked her the question that was on her mind, "What are we going to do?"

"Pray Rebecca and Elias are better tomorrow. If not, and the captain goes through with his threat, we must go ashore and take care of them."

Avram nodded his agreement. "I am astonished the captain gives credence to a pagan god." He wrung out the cloth that rested on Elias's face, dipping it in wine and replacing it. "I will go and see what I can find out from the sailors."

Channah's mind raced while she dabbed wine on Rebecca's feverish brow. She had no idea how far they had come nor how much distance still separated them from Ephesus. How would she pay for the remaining passage when her friends recovered? She tried to pray, but could find few words. *Help us, Lord Jesus. We are strangers in a strange land.*

The sound of Miriam playing with the babies on the other side of their makeshift privacy barrier reminded Channah she must not sink into despair. The children depended on her, and she had to be strong for them.

After a while, Avram returned, bringing her dried fish from the store of food Dorcas had packed for them. "Seleucia Pieria, the port the captain mentioned, is on the outskirts of the city of Antioch. They have a Jewish quarter there called Kerateion. I am not sure I said that right." He nibbled at his fish. "The sailor told me the captain is the main one who worships the Roman goddess Fortuna. However, all of them are somewhat superstitious about shipboard illness and death."

Channah glanced at Rebecca's contorted face. "Surely, this is a short-term plague. They must recover."

Avram dropped his eyes. "They are gravely ill, both of them."

"But what of Julia?" Channah knew the answer even while she asked the question. "What will we do with her?"

"As you have done with Miriam and I did with you." Avram shrugged. "The best we can."

During the night, Elias stopped moaning and twitching. Channah could not awaken him to urge him to take a swallow of wine. His shallow breathing was the only confirmation he was still alive. Rebecca opened her eyes, but quickly shut them, groaned, and turned away from nourishment.

The ship captain came and stared at the two people on the sleeping mat, and then walked away without speaking.

"As soon as I nurse the babies, we must go and pack our belongings," she told Miriam.

"No, Ima. Uncle and I did that already. Everything is ready except for the sleeping mats.

Channah hugged her daughter. "Thank you. I do not know what I would do without you, my sweet girl."

"I like helping you, Ima. I helped Uncle on the island."

"Yes, you did. You are very brave." *May I have half the courage of my child.*

"What are we going to do when we get off the ship?" Miriam's tone conveyed more curiosity than apprehension.

"I am not certain." Channah laid Julia on a mat and eased her other breast out of Joshua's mouth. "God will show us the way."

Avram came into their space breathing heavily. “I have spoken with the captain again. He is determined to put Elias and Rebecca off the ship. He plans to be in port for several hours to unload his cargo and take on another load. I will go and find us lodging in the Jewish quarter of the city. Then I will return and take us there.”

“Good plan.” Channah nodded, grateful for her uncle’s willingness to scout the unfamiliar city.

“I will go now,” Avram said. “I want to be the first man off the ship when it settles into the harbor.”

“Here.” Channah held out a pouch of coins Dorcas pressed into her hand at Joppa. “You may need this.”

Shortly after Avram walked away, Miriam asked, “Surely, he will not desert us. Will he?”

“Of course not,” Channah assured her daughter. “As long as there is life in his body, Uncle Avram will not forsake us.”

Chapter Thirty-Seven

"I cannot wait for the old man any longer," the captain told Channah. "Everyone going ashore must go now." He nodded toward the mats where Elias and Rebecca lay like corpses. "My men are coming to put them off the ship. I need the space they are occupying for the rest of my cargo."

Channah stood and faced him. "My children and I are prepared to go. We need help carrying our belongings."

"Your possessions are not my responsibility," the captain said. "I have a ship to manage, and I have already been unnecessarily delayed waiting for your father to return."

Not bothering to explain that Avram was her uncle, Channah picked up Joshua. "Bring Julia," she told Miriam. She followed the captain across the deck. Raising her voice, she declared, "You have no right to cut our journey short because of your superstition."

The captain turned and regarded her with surprise written on his face. "I am in authority—"

Summoning her courage, Channah interrupted him. "You have been paid to take my family all the way to Ephesus. Since you are forcing us to go ashore here, the least you can do is to make sure our baggage gets off the ship with us." She took a deep breath, attempting to control her anger. "If you do not bring my possessions ashore, I will notify Dorcas that you put us off the ship early and kept our belongings."

"Dorcas?" questioned one of the crew. "The woman at Joppa who gives food and clothing to shipwrecked sailors?"

"Yes." Channah's knees were feeling weak. "That is the one. She will warn everyone in Joppa not to do business with you."

"And just how would you get such a message from Syria to Joppa?" the captain sneered.

She repeated something she heard Elias say before he became ill. "The Roman Empire has a very efficient postal system."

Addressing the sailor who asked about Dorcas, the captain said, "You. Get these people and everything they own off my ship immediately."

With the assistance of two sailors, Channah soon found herself standing on a white, sandy beach. She clung to Joshua's hand, while Miriam held Julia. Rebecca and Elias lay on their sleeping mats. The chest containing weaving tools and supplies would have provided a sitting place, except for having food and clothing piled on its top.

"Do not stray," she admonished Joshua. She spread her traveling cloak over Rebecca and Elias to keep them from being burned by the sun. With no coins, there was no possibility of patronizing the dockside food vendors. She was digging through her possessions for something to eat when two men strolling along the beach wandered near.

Joshua accosted them. "Are you my abba?" he demanded.

"Joshua!" Channah was mortified. She ran to grab her son.

With a chuckle, the men greeted Joshua and walked on. She could only hope they did not understand the boy's embarrassing question. For the moment, she was glad to be among people who spoke a different language.

Channah sat between Rebecca and Elias and leaned against the weaver's chest, watching the children play. She was too weary to care that Joshua was filling her cooking pot with sand.

If her uncle did not come soon, she had to figure out shelter for the night. She struggled to keep from accepting the warm sun's invitation to fall asleep. *Have mercy on us, Lord Jesus. Help us.*

Through half-closed eyes, Channah spied Avram walking toward the wharf. "Uncle," she called out.

He instantly turned and came toward her. "I was alarmed when I saw the ship was gone." He squatted near Joshua and put a hand on the boy's head. "Thank God you are safe. I have good news."

"I cook soup." Joshua held out a handful of wet sand.

"Yes, I see. It looks delicious." Avram stood and brushed sand from his tunic. "It took longer than I expected to locate the synagogue. Antioch is bigger than I ever imagined a city could be." He gestured away from the sea. "A follower of the Way is allowing us to sleep in his stable while Elias and his wife recover. He has sent his cart and driver to take us there."

The cart bed was large enough for Rebecca and Elias to lie stretched out full length on their mats. They gave no sign of consciousness when Avram and the driver hoisted them onto the cart. Channah and the children took places around the sick couple among the baggage. Once the cart was packed and the back gate closed, the high sides blocked Channah's view. Joshua wiggled in her lap. Miriam had a firm grasp on Julia, who placidly sucked her thumb.

As they rode to the city, Channah considered what essentials had to be done before they could lie down and sleep. She was too exhausted to think beyond today.

Channah supposed they must be at their destination when the cart stopped. As soon as she relaxed her hold on Joshua, he began to climb the cart's side. "No," she said, pulling him back toward her. "You will fall."

Two strangers pulled open the cart's back gate. "Welcome," a woman with a round face said. "I am Eliana. We are here to help you get settled for the evening."

After introductions, Channah asked, "Do you know of anyone who can help the sick couple?"

"The Jewish doctors are observing the Sabbath today," Eliana replied. "My husband brought our son's friend, who is studying to be a physician."

With a crew of men working steadily, the cart was quickly unloaded. Their possessions were neatly stacked in the corner of a large, open area in the spacious stable. Each sleeping mat rested on a fat pallet of fresh straw.

Eliana served a rich vegetable stew and fresh bread. It was the first hot food Channah had eaten since boarding the ship, and it seemed to her she never tasted anything better. Eliana tried to feed Rebecca, but without success.

The serious young man who was studying medicine knelt and examined Elias. After a moment, he stood and shook his head. "They are beyond anything I know. I will ask my teacher to come." With those words, he quickly exited the open stable door.

"Is there anything we can do to make you more comfortable?" Eliana asked after clearing away the remains of the evening meal.

"I cannot think of a thing." Channah was still tired, but food and the assurance of a place to sleep comforted her. "How can we ever thank you enough for your kindness?"

“My family is honored to be of assistance.” She hugged Channah. “Avram got directions to the meeting place for the followers of the Way. Perhaps when your friends recover, you will be able to join us in worship.”

“Thank you. I would like very much to do so.”

Eliana beckoned to her husband and sons. “All right, boys. It is time to pray over our new friends. Then we will go home and let these folks get some rest.”

After dark, there was a rap on the barn door. “Yes?” Avram called out.

“It is Luke. I have brought Doctor Stratis.”

Avram quickly admitted the young man and the distinguished-looking gentleman with him. The physician wasted no time. “Where are the patients?”

Avram led the way, while Channah lit an oil lamp. She stood over Elias, holding the light for the doctor.

“See here? The fingernails?” Stratis muttered to Luke. “That is always something to check.” He poked at Elias’s stomach and looked his body over before turning to Rebecca. After a time, he declared, “She has the same illness as her husband, poor woman. By the way, has her leg been this way from birth, or was she in an accident?”

“We have not known them long,” Avram said. “We do not know how she became lame.”

“No matter.” Doctor Stratis sat cross-legged on the sleeping mat. “Has everyone in this group eaten the same food at the same time over the past few days?”

“No,” Avram answered. “We boarded a ship in Joppa. It stopped at many towns along the coast. Sometimes, we went ashore and obtained food separately.”

“When did they fall ill?”

"Not long after we left Acco," Avram replied. "I believe the man was sick first, and his wife later."

Channah nodded her agreement.

"And no one else among you has any symptoms?"

"No. Not even their child."

"Where is he?"

"She," he corrected himself, as soon as Channah fetched Julia from her own mat. He took the sleeping baby, holding her with one arm and feeling of her face, hands, feet, and stomach, with the other. "The child appears to be healthy." He handed her back to Channah. "That is more than I can say for these two," He waved an arm over Elias and Rebecca. "My guess is poison berries. They are ripening along the coast now, and many of them look similar to perfectly harmless varieties. The man and woman will reach a crisis soon, possibly tonight or tomorrow. At that point, each will begin a lengthy recovery, or they will die." He met Channah's eyes. "I am sorry. They are young. Perhaps there is hope. The only consolation I can offer is that they have nothing contagious. If you bought dried berries along the way, let the birds can have them. They can digest food humans cannot."

Channah stepped outside the stable at dawn. She yawned and stretched her arms. As the physician predicted, Elias and Rebecca's fever burned into the night. During the wee hours of the morning, Elias stopped breathing. Rebecca moaned and thrashed on her mat, but she was still alive.

Channah became aware of Avram's presence beside her. "Have you slept at all?" he asked.

"A little."

"You should go and get some rest before the children awaken."

"Uncle, Elias has passed from this life into the next."

"I know." He munched on bread left from their last evening meal. "The Lord's ways are mysterious. Why would he take a young believer like Elias and leave a broken-down old man like me still breathing?"

She slipped her arm around his waist. "I hope you know how grateful I am to have you with me. I truly do not know what I would do without you."

"As I am thankful for you, little one." He cleared his throat. "I will attend the Way meeting this morning. Surely someone in the congregation will help us bury Elias. Then tomorrow, I must see if there is any work for an old shepherd in this wealthy city."

"I would love to work with you, Uncle, but I must care for Rebecca and the children."

"Naturally." Avram nodded.

"Perhaps I can earn something as a weaver." She yawned again. "I wonder how long it will be before we can resume our journey. Some days I fear we will never get to Ephesus."

"Based on information from our host Manaen, I estimate it will take several months, but less than a year to earn passage on a ship to Ephesus."

"Is walking on the roads not a possibility?"

"There are some formidable mountains between Antioch and Ephesus, often right down to the edge of the sea. Manaen told me we would have great difficulty taking the land route. Besides," he glanced toward the barn, "consider how difficult walking must be for Rebecca and Miriam."

She sighed. "Joshua may be a grown man before we reach our destination."

"And perhaps then he will no longer ask every man he meets if he is his abba."

She wrinkled her brow. Avram was not on the beach when Joshua accosted the men from Antioch. "Have you seen him do this?"

Avram smiled. "Yes, Manaen, and then each of his sons last evening."

"Oh, no." Channah clapped a hand to her head. "I suppose I said we are going to find his father too many times before we left Joppa. I must warn him to stop speaking to strangers."

Chapter Thirty-Eight

Channah lifted Rebecca's head and pushed straw under her mat to keep her almost upright. "Food will help you regain your strength." She dipped bread into the broth and popped the sop into Rebecca's mouth.

Rebecca chewed slowly and swallowed. "Mmm. Good." Her eyes moved left and right "Where am I?"

"We are in the city of Antioch. You became so ill we had to leave the ship."

"Where is Elias?" Rebecca took another look around.

"My uncle pulled his mat into an empty stall." Channah dreaded breaking the news that this poor young woman's husband was dead.

"Is Julia all right?"

"Yes, my dear. She is outside with Miriam and Joshua. Please try to eat."

"No more," Rebecca said after a few more bites. "The bread and broth tastes better than anything I can ever remember. But I am too tired to take any more nourishment." She closed her eyes. "Thank you."

"You are most welcome." Channah readjusted the mat so Rebecca was again prone. She pulled the blanket up to her chin. "There now. Rest a while. Do not fret over Julia. Miriam is taking good care of her."

"Is Elias dead?" Rebecca asked without opening her eyes.

"Yes. He is."

"When?"

"Last night. I am so sorry."

"Thank you for telling me the truth." Tears crept from beneath her closed eyelids, but she made no further sound for a long moment. “His family was the only one in our village who would consider making a marriage contract for a lame girl. And that was only because my father offered a fat dowry.” She opened her eyes and turned her head toward Channah. “My father-in-law disowned Elias when we began to follow the Way. He took my dowry and cast us out. That was wrong of him.”

Channah patted her hand. “It is hard to find justice in this world. You must rest.”

“Yes.” Rebecca turned on her side. “I will sleep now.”

Channah wished she, too, could collapse onto her mat and sleep. Instead, she opened the big wooden chest and rifled through the contents. She pulled out the pieces and assembled the frame of her loom. She decided to do a plain tabby pattern for the sake of speed. It took a while to get the warp strings attached and the tension adjusted exactly the same for each string.

After checking on the children, Channah filled her shuttle and began to weave. She had worked steadily in Dorcas’s work room. Now, with children and a sick woman to care for, she realized she would be constantly interrupted. However, she hoped to have a single length of fabric done by the end of the following day.

Avram returned from the meeting bearing loaves of bread. “Eliana sent this.”

“Your face is bruised.” Channah accepted the bread. “And your hand is bleeding. What happened to you? Was there trouble at the worship gathering?”

“It is nothing.” Avram wiped his hand with a rag. “I tripped over a stump on the way home.”

Channah took the rag from him, poured wine on it, and dabbed at his hand. “It is not a deep cut.”

“I am getting clumsy in my old age.”

Miriam kissed Avram's hand, and said, "There are too many clouds in the sky today."

Avram frowned.

"Clouds?" Channah was puzzled. "What have clouds to do with stumbling?"

Miriam ducked her head and chewed her bottom lip. When she glanced at Avram, he shook his head.

Channah gently lifted her daughter's chin and gazed into her eyes. "Tell me about the clouds."

"They make it hard for Uncle to see." Miriam leaned against Avram. "He needs bright light." Once the child began to speak, she could not seem to stop. "On the island, I had to be his eyes except when the sun was very bright. He could not spot ships in the distance. So, I had to look for them."

"Uncle." Channah turned to Avram. "I had no idea."

"Eyes grow dim with old age. Everyone knows that." He shrugged. "I did not want to worry you."

Miriam looked to be close to tears. "I am sorry I told, Uncle."

"Your ima was bound to notice sooner or later." He pressed Miriam against his side. "You did nothing wrong."

While Channah absorbed the information about Avram's eyesight, he took the conversation in another direction.

"A man named Nicholas has arranged for Elias's burial. Also, two families on their way to Macedonia will sleep in the other end of the stable this evening."

"Let me tell you about this morning's meeting. It was glorious. Did you know the Apostle Peter once traveled here to Antioch? He spoke in the synagogue. Manaen and Eliana were among the Jews who believed in Jesus because of the apostle's preaching. Since then, many of their Gentile neighbors have also become believers. They do not refer to themselves as followers of the Way, however. They call themselves Christians.'

"Christians. I like the sound of it." Channah smoothed Miriam's hair, not wishing her to be upset at revealing Avram's secret.

"So do I," Avram agreed. "Because the name immediately acknowledges Christ, while saying 'the Way' does not. I also found out why there are no animals in this stable."

Miriam spoke up. "Why?"

"This land belongs to a Greek Cypriot named Joseph. Peter, his wife, and several families traveling with them lodged here. Afterward, Joseph asked Manaen to look after the place for him. So now, believers can stay here when they are passing through Antioch. Manaen said Joseph has plans to build a house here eventually."

"The apostle slept here, in this very stable? Did I tell you he stayed with a tanner in Joppa? He is a man of great humility."

"I only met him once." Avram wiped a few drops of blood from the scratch on his hand. "I never saw a man more passionate about his faith."

Miriam seemed to be unimpressed. "I wish there was a donkey in this stable. I could pet it."

Chapter Thirty-Nine

In two weeks' time, Rebecca had enough strength to help care for the children. After a month in the stable, she took over the cooking as well. She proved to be a frugal manager of their food budget, often bartering Channah's bread for fresh vegetables.

Against Avram's feeble protests, Channah sent Miriam with him to the fields to be his eyes while he worked as a shepherd. "I like being outside with the sheep," the girl told Channah. "The flock knows me now, and they follow me as well as they do Uncle. I want to be a shepherd woman when I grow up." She paused, then asked, "Do they have sheep in Ephesus?"

"Yes," Channah answered. "I am certain they do. That is one reason your abba chose that city. He knew we would find work there."

"Are we ever going to see Abba again?"

Channah stopped weaving long enough to hug her daughter. "I pray that we will."

"But it has been so long. Maybe he has forgotten about us."

"No. Love is longsuffering."

"What does that mean?"

"I suppose it means not forgetting about those you love, no matter how long you are separated."

Channah often worked into the night, weaving by the light of an oil lamp. Her projects were finished swiftly, since she did not have to spend time preparing fibers or spinning. Dorcas had sent an ample supply of finished twine in the trunk she packed.

At the end of four months, Avram counted out their coins after the evening meal. "At this rate, we will soon have enough to buy passage on a ship going to Ephesus."

"How much more do we need?" Channah asked.

When Avram told her, she said, "Tomorrow I will sell my extra tunics, those Dorcas sent. They are very fine and should bring a good price. With that, plus the length of cloth I finished this afternoon, we should be able to continue our journey."

Rebecca, who seldom spoke unless directly addressed, said, "Please, will you sell my cloak as well? And Elias's things?"

"Certainly, men's clothing is much in demand. Perhaps you should keep your cloak for the chilly evenings on the ship."

"You have worked so hard for our passage. I must contribute something." Rebecca lowered her eyes. "Or, I can remain here if you do not wish for me to go on with you."

Channah moved next to Rebecca and put an arm around the young woman's shoulders. "Of course, we want you to go with us. That is, unless you prefer to stay in Antioch."

"What is there for you here?" Avram asked.

"Nothing," Rebecca replied. "I have no husband, no money, no skills. I only have Julia, and I do not know how I shall be able to provide for her. I am worthless."

"That is not true," Channah said. "You are a pearl of great price because you belong to Jesus. I will teach you what I know about weaving if you like. Or shepherding."

"Thank you. I must learn some trade. No man will marry a lame widow with no skills and no family."

"I will be your family," Miriam offered.

Rebecca began to weep. "Thank you."

"As head of this household," Avram said, "I declare that we are a family unit, all of us. Channah and Rebecca, you are my daughters. Joshua, Miriam, and Julia are my grandchildren. So be it, henceforth and forevermore. Amen."

"I have always wanted a sister." Channah gave Rebecca a side hug. "Let us gather our goods for tomorrow's market."

Three days later, after many good-byes and expressions of thanks to the Christians of Antioch, the newly-formed family boarded a ship bound for Ephesus.

"Lord willing, we will be in our new home in a few days." Avram said, as they watched the coastline slip away.

Yes, Channah thought. *May God grant us no sickness nor shipwrecks, nor delays of any kind. May he give us work to earn a living. May he guide us to John Simon.*

As she anticipated, Channah was seasick the better part of the first day at sea. She consoled herself with the vow she would never again leave dry land once they reached Ephesus. When she recovered, she passed the time teaching Rebecca how to make twine using a spindle.

Avram paced the deck, often led by Miriam or Joshua, proudly claiming them and Julia as his grandchildren. He often engaged the sailors in conversation, and then reported whatever he learned to the women he called his daughters.

Chapter Forty

Sitting around the campfire after the evening meal, watching the dusk fade into darkness used to be Channah's favorite time of day. Since settling near Ephesus a week ago, she dreaded the nightly admonition from Avram.

He uncle spoke gently. "You must let me find you a husband."

"Please, let us not have this discussion again. John Simon is my husband."

"You must be realistic. My eyesight grows dimmer all the time, and I feel a weakness in my legs. The day is coming when I cannot come to the fields with you. Then what?"

"Then you can rest in our tent. Or go into the city and pass time with the old men who play backgammon in the marketplace. Rebecca and I can tend the sheep. Miriam is a big help, and eventually Joshua and Julia will learn. How long has Auntie been dead? Yet you have never spoken of taking another wife."

"It is different for me, because I am a man. No matter than I have grown half-blind and weak. Who was able to negotiate our employment with Ali Allisad? Would he have considered letting two women and three children shepherd his fat-tailed sheep out here in a remote pasture? Of course not. That would be an invitation to robbers. Or worse."

"Rebecca has told me she is willing to remarry."

Avram stared into his cup for a long moment, the way he did when he had something unpleasant to say. "It is a daunting task to find a man willing to marry a sickly lame woman. You on the other hand are healthy and strong, and you have a trade."

Obviously, Avram did not see Rebecca standing nearby in the twilight. Channah winced, but her friend made a dismissive hand motion to indicate she was not offended.

"I appreciate your loyalty to John Simon," Avram continued. "However, you must consider your children. Miriam and Joshua need a father to protect and care for them. What if you become ill or Rebecca has an injury? Furthermore, you have no one to make sure Joshua gets an education."

He had attacked her greatest vulnerability, her children's future. Nevertheless, she was determined not to consider taking another husband unless she saw John Simon's lifeless body for herself. Why could her uncle not accept her decision and let the matter rest? Channah's response was a quiet "No."

"I will go into Ephesus tomorrow," Avram announced.

"Why is that?" Channah asked.

"I have business to do. Something a woman would not understand, even if I explained it."

Channah glanced at Rebecca, whose face wore a surprised expression. "Then Miriam must go with you."

Avram was uncharacteristically brusque. "I am not blind yet." He stood and began to stomp away, but stumbled and fell to his knees.

"Miriam will be your eyes," Channah gently insisted. "She will keep you from being run over by the carts on the city streets."

Without acknowledging Channah's words, Avram went to a spot in the midst of the sheep where he liked to make his bed. He shook out his blanket and sat with his back to the women.

"Why is our father angry?" Rebecca asked.

"I think he must be afraid for us because he is losing his eyesight." Channah put away her mending, lacking sufficient light to continue.

Rebecca pulled at her headscarf. "I hope I have not said or done something to offend him."

"No," Channah assured her. "He has not been himself lately. I wonder what business he has in Ephesus." She shrugged. "We will know soon enough. Miriam will tell me everything when they get home."

The next morning, Avram and Miriam left for the city before sunrise.

"Where are we going?" the girl asked while leading the old man along the pathway to the river.

"I am going to consult a physician, but I do not want your ima to know about it. She would only worry."

"Is he going to heal your eyes?"

Instead of a yes or no, Avram merely grunted.

At the river, they took a rowboat ferry to the opposite bank. Avram questioned the young man with a patch over his eye about local doctors. As the man spoke, Miriam repeated his instructions on where to find the physician's house. After they reached the outskirts of the city, she followed the memorized directions to take Avram where he wanted to go.

A slender, clean-shaven man answered the door with a quiet "Shalom."

"Shalom," Avram replied. "Are you doctor Caleb?"

"I am. Please come in." The man glanced from Avram to Miriam. "Which of you is the patient?"

"I am."

"Come with me." The doctor turned toward a hallway. "The girl may wait in the courtyard."

In a small room, Doctor Caleb motioned toward a low bed. "Sit down." He took a seat on a stool next to the bed. "There is no cure for old-age blindness," he said without any preface. "It comes upon everyone who lives long enough."

"It is not my eyesight that concerns me." Avram lifted his tunic. "I have a hard lump in my abdomen. It is growing."

The doctor felt the growth and the entire area around it. When Avram winced, he asked, "Is it painful?"

"Yes."

"Always, or only when I press?"

"All the time, somewhat," Avram said. "More so when you poke on me. I know I have a cancer, doctor. And I am certain it is fatal. My only question is this. How long will I survive?"

"That is hard to say. Your tumor is quite advanced. Perhaps only a few weeks. At the most, half a year. I can give you treatments, but I must tell you I have had no success curing or even slowing down these terrible growths."

"I have already lived many more years than any man should ask." Avram pulled his tunic down. "My soul and spirit will return to God after leaving this decrepit body, and that is more than enough for me. There is only one matter of unfinished business I must attend to, and that is to find husbands to take care of my daughters when I am gone. Do you know of a good Jewish matchmaker in Ephesus?"

"The best one is a woman called Thalia. She lives not far from here."

"Thank you." Avram stood and adjusted his clothing. "I will not trouble you further. Shalom, my friend."

In the vestibule, Avram felt his way by holding onto the wall. He was relieved when Miriam took hold of his hand.

"Shall we go home now?"

"No, child, I must make another stop first. It is to the left, two streets over, and then the second house on the right side. Can you guide me there?"

"Yes. Left, two streets over. Second house on the right."

"Good." He squeezed her hand.

As Miriam led him along, Avram said, "I want you to promise me you will not tell your ima the places where we go today."

"Why is that?"

"I want to give her a gift. If you tell her anything about today, you will spoil the surprise."

They walked further before Miriam spoke again. "Jesus does not want me to lie to my ima."

"If she asks where we went, you must tell her that you promised not to tell. She will not make you break a vow. Will you do that for me?"

"Yes, Uncle. I mean, Grandfather. I will keep your secret." She stopped. "We are at the door of the house you want."

Chapter Forty-One

After a brief wait in the matchmaker's courtyard, a young woman appeared. "Thalia will see you now."

Avram patted Miriam's head. "Wait here for me, little one. I should not be long."

Once inside, it was difficult for him to navigate the house's dark passageways. "Would you mind leading me?" He asked the young woman. "My eyesight has grown dim."

"Yes. I understand." She did not move forward until he laid his hand on her shoulder. He followed her closely until they entered a room with enough sunlight for him to see.

"Well, good morning. I am Thalia, the matchmaker." The woman at the writing table had a round bosom and even rounder belly. "Please be seated. How may I serve you today?"

"I want to arrange marriages for my two daughters."

Thalia took a reed pen and dipped it in ink. "Where do you live?"

"Here, in Ephesus."

She stared at him. "You are Jewish?"

"Yes."

"How is it possible you live in my city and have two daughters eligible to be married, and I have not heard of you?"

"We are new here," Avram explained. "I said we live in the city. Actually, we have just now settled in an outlying pasture, tending the sheep of Ali Allisad. His brother-in-law is a merchant. I met him on the ship coming in to Ephesus. He knew Ali needed a shepherd. One thing led to another. My family went straight from the dock to the fields."

"I know of Ali Allisad. He is an Arab who tries to be Jewish."

"He is a follower of the Way, if that is what you mean. My daughters and I are Jesus worshipers as well. They called us Christians in Antioch."

"I call you...never mind. I suppose like all members of this sect, you want your daughters to have husbands of the same belief."

"Yes, that is the most important consideration."

She sighed. "That narrows the possibilities, but I love a challenge. Tell me about your daughters. Hopefully, they are beautiful, young virgins capable of earning wages and bearing children." Thalia poised her reed pen over a sheet of papyrus.

"They are young widows, both of them in their early twenties. Rebecca is very fair of face, with a lame right leg. She has a three-year-old adopted daughter and plans to learn to be a shepherdess." He cleared his throat. "Her child is a gentile."

"Lame," Thalia muttered. "No skill, wants a husband who follows the Way." After she stopped writing, she made eye contact with Avram. "And the other one?"

"She may be difficult to match."

Thalia rolled her eyes. "Worse than the one-legged widow with a gentile daughter? This should be interesting."

"Channah is not convinced her husband is dead, although it has been more than four years since we have heard from him. She really does not wish to remarry."

"And so you will force her?"

"No. I hope to convince her," Avram replied. "For her own sake and her children."

"I see." Thalia wrote again. "You do realize that my service fee is based on finding a suitable match, even if the result is not marriage."

"I do."

"Describe your daughter."

"Channah is even-tempered and kind to everyone. Her faith is unwavering. Excepting for my dear wife Yael, may she rest in peace, Channah is the best shepherd I have ever known. She has a young daughter and a son who was born after we were separated from John Simon in a shipwreck. She also bakes the best bread this side of Heaven."

"John Simon and Channah. Why do those names sound familiar? Have you been to Ephesus before?"

"No, never. John Simon was Channah's husband's name."

She reached to a nearby shelf and set a box on her table. "Where are you from?"

"We recently spent a few months in Antioch, but we are originally from the hills around Bethlehem."

Thalia opened the wooden box and removed a stack of papyrus sheets. She removed the top leaf, then the others one-by-one, slowly. "Ah." She re-stacked everything, and returned all but one sheet to the box. "Suppose for a moment that this John Simon is alive. Would that information be worth the same price as making a match?"

"Yes, definitely. Nothing would make me happier. Do you know something about him?"

The matchmaker smiled. "I have many resources. I may be able to discover whether he is yet among the living." Her eyes dropped to the one remaining page before her. "Are your daughters adopted by any chance?" She smiled again. "I mean to say, it appears adoption is common in your family."

"Yes." Avram nodded. "In terms of blood, Channah is my great niece. We met Rebecca on the way to Antioch. After her husband died, she had no one. So, we took her into our family." He paused at Thalia's giggle. "Have I said something amusing?"

"No." She covered her mouth and coughed. "Not at all. I seem to have a tickle in my throat." She set aside the papyrus that came from the box. "I will write out a contract. You can read, I presume."

"Yes."

"Good. All you need to do is sign and pay half of my price. The remainder is due when I find matches for your daughters." She pretended to cough again, obviously covering laughter. "Which I suspect will be very soon. Very soon indeed."

Within a few minutes, Thalia led Avram to her courtyard, where Miriam sat patiently waiting.

He beckoned to her. "Come, little one. Let us go."

After they exited the house, Miriam asked, "Shall we go to the river now?"

"After one more stop. If you can find us a bakery, we will buy treats to take home for everyone."

"I saw a bakery not far from here. Shall I guide you there?"

"Yes." Avram gave her his hand. "As the prophet said, 'a little child shall lead them'." He chuckled. "Honey cakes are your favorite, are they not?"

"They are, but ima says they cost too much at the bakery."

“She is correct,” Avram agreed. “However, today we shall ignore the cost.”

“Is today special?”

“Every day is special,” Avram tilted his head toward the sky. “Life is God’s gift, and we should thank him by celebrating every single day of it.”

Chapter Forty-Two

Channah stopped braiding Rebecca's hair long enough to check on the lentil and bean soup cooking over the campfire. "Stay still. I will be right back." She stirred and tasted the soup. "Good." Returning to where Rebecca sat like a statue on a tree stump, she finished off the braid and tied it with a ribbon.

"I hope he likes me," Rebecca fretted.

"How could he not?" Channah asked.

Rebecca patted her new hairdo. "Many of our people believe my lame leg is punishment for some sin I committed, or something my parents did."

"The followers of Jesus do not accept that belief," Channah assured her. "And Uncle—I mean Father—said he told the matchmaker you would only consider marrying a devout follower of the Way. Besides, this meeting is only for you to get acquainted with each other. If you sense anything amiss, you are not required to betroth yourself to Alexander."

"I wonder how old he is." Rebecca wrapped a sash around her tunic. "Thank you for weaving a new belt for me."

"I wish I could have made you a new tunic," Channah said as she pulled a comb through her hair. "There just was not enough time."

"Yes," Rebecca agreed. "Father spoke to the matchmaker only two weeks ago, and already we have an encounter set. Where is Julia? I must put this ribbon in her hair."

"Miriam is helping with the sheep, and as you know, Joshua and Julia follow her around the way chicks trail after a mother hen."

By midafternoon, everything was in readiness. Fresh bread was ready for baking, the children were dressed, and the sheep were quietly grazing within eyesight. Joshua and Julia ran and played. Everyone else sat in awkward silence.

At last, two men and a woman veered from the pathway to the river to approach the pasture. “Is that the young man who rows the ferry?” Channah asked while the three people were still out of earshot.

“Yes,” Miriam piped up. “It is.”

The adults rose and went to meet the approaching visitors.

According to protocol, Avram spoke first. “Welcome to our home. I am Avram.” He waved his arm toward the women. “My daughters, Channah and Rebecca.”

“Shalom. My name is Zimri. My son, Alexander. My wife, Sarah.”

Rebecca and Alexander exchanged glances before both dropped their eyes and blushed.

Zimri put a hand on his son’s shoulder. “We should take a stroll through this lush pastureland. Perhaps Avram and Rebecca would care to join us?”

“May I go too, Ima?” Joshua asked.

“Not this time.” Channah took the boy’s hand as a precaution. “Let us show Sarah to our tent.”

“Most gracious,” Sarah murmured.

The women and children went toward the tent, with Joshua looking back at every opportunity. “Is that man with one eye my abba?” he asked.

Channah knelt and took her son’s face in her hands. “You are not to think every man you meet is your abba. How many times have I told you this?”

Joshua scowled. “I am sorry.”

Little Julia hugged Joshua. “Friends,” was all she said.

Channah turned to Sarah. “Forgive my son’s manners. He cannot forget that I told him we came to Ephesus to find his father.”

“I understand.” Sarah smiled. “Boys will be boys.”

Near the cooking fire, Miriam unstacked serving trays.

“Where are you from?” Sarah asked.

The abrupt question took Channah by surprise. “I was born in Jerusalem and lived there for a few years. After I was orphaned, my great uncle and his wife raised me in the Bethlehem hills.” Channah kept her eyes on Rebecca.

Avram and Zimri went a short distance into the herd of sheep and stopped. Alexander and Rebecca went about a stone’s throw further.

“I do not see any family resemblance between you and your sister.” Sarah motioned to the young couple, who now appeared to be engaged in deep conversation. “Do the two of you have the same father and mother?”

Channah briefly explained how Rebecca became a member of her family.”

“What about you? Are you a widow also?”

The barrage of prying questions rankled Channah. *I am not the prospective bride.* Nevertheless, she patiently explained that she nurtured the hope of finding John Simon.

“John Simon? That is your husband’s name?” Sarah asked.

“Yes.” Channah stirred her cooking pot, still watching Rebecca. She strained to observe any possible clue to the couple’s reactions. Body language suggested the conversation between Rebecca and Alexander was going well.

Sarah’s eyes were trained on her son. “Alexander likes your sister.”

“You know this already?”

“Yes,” Sarah said. “I can tell by the way he stands with his hands behind his back. He may not say it, but a mother knows. How did she become lame?”

“She told me she was born that way.” Channah arranged loaves of bread on the serving trays. “She cannot run or walk a great distance, but she is a hard worker. Very reliable. And she is a good ima to Julia.”

“Ah, yes, the little girl with the beautiful golden curls.” Sarah patted Julia’s head. “How did Rebecca find this sweet child?”

Channah told the story of Dorcas and her kindness. “Dorcas thought it best for the baby to leave Israel because of the persecution. So, Rebecca and her husband were good enough to adopt her.”

“What happened to the first husband?”

Although there was no need for additional firewood, Channah sent Miriam in search of some anyway. She knew Joshua and Julia would follow the older girl. When the children were some distance away, Channah recounted the story of the poison berries and the family’s stay in Antioch.

At last Zimri made a beckoning motion toward Sarah. Without comment, she rose and went to where he stood. Alexander joined them. Meanwhile, Avram and Rebecca came toward Channah.

Avram immediately sat on the ground. “Ah, this feels good. I was tired of standing.”

Channah and Rebecca sat near him, forming a small circle. Out of the corner of her eye, Channah saw Miriam returning. “Take Joshua to the tent and wash his face,” Channah said.

Miriam inspected her little brother. “His face is clean, Ima.”

“Take him among the sheep, then, and keep him busy for a while. This is an adult conversation.”

With a frown, Miriam led Joshua away. Julia wore an uncertain expression, but soon followed the other two children.

“The father seems to be a decent fellow,” Avram said. “Although he asked many pointless questions.”

“The mother is very inquisitive also,” Channah agreed. “Not the worst fault a mother-in-law can have, I suppose.”

Abram hunched forward. “What do you think of Alexander, Rebecca?”

The blush that rose to the young woman’s face revealed the answer before she spoke. “I like him. Very much.” She blushed brighter and ducked her head.

“Are you willing to be his wife? You do not have to decide right away, if you feel you need more time.”

Rebecca’s eyes were fixed on her folded hands, but her voice was strong. “I am willing.” She made eye contact with Channah and then Avram. “His faith is strong and seems to be real. Because of his blind eye, I feel he has compassion for me. Not pity, more like an understanding of what it is like to be different. He said he would pitch a tent for us near yours if you agree. That would allow me to continue learning about sheep. And to remain with the family I have come to love.”

"Good." Avram wrapped his arms around his knees. "Zimri and I will set a wedding date as soon as young Alexander gets your tent put up."

The trio sat in silence, each one of them occasionally glancing at the other family group.

"I thought he liked me," Rebecca said at last. "What is taking them so long?"

Channah mentally reviewed her conversation with the mother, wondering if she had inadvertently said something that offended her.

"It may be they are cautious." Avram stared at Zimri's back. "Some people take more time to come to a decision than others."

"Or perhaps I misjudged him. Perhaps he does not want a lame wife."

Channah slipped her arm over Rebecca's shoulders. "If that is true of Alexander, you are better off without him."

At last, Zimri walked to where Avram sat. "Avram, I would like for us to work out the specifics of a marriage contract between my son, Alexander, and your daughter, Rebecca."

Avram struggled to stand. "You honor my house with this proposal. I will be most pleased to give my daughter to your son. Will you join us in a meal?"

Channah, Rebecca, and Miriam sprang up and began final preparations to serve the food.

Zimri shuffled his feet and cleared his throat. "My son and I would like to speak with you in regards to another matter. Privately, if we may."

With a quizzical look, Avram gestured to the open pasture. "Please."

Channah stirred the stew, wondering whether she should go ahead and fill the serving trays or not. She saw a worried look on Rebecca's face. However, Sarah's presence restrained her from speculating aloud on the men's conversation. "I suppose I should wait until they return to ladle the soup," she said.

Sarah smiled and shrugged, but offered no affirmative or negative response.

Desperate to fill the silence, Channah asked, "Sarah, are you fond of weaving?"

"Not in particular."

After other futile attempts at conversation failed, Channah gave up. Not knowing what else to do, she stirred the soup until she heard her name being called.

Avram was motioning her to come to the clearing where he sat with Zimri and Alexander.

"Something must be wrong," she said as she dropped her wooden spoon.

"No," Sarah said, smiling. "All is well."

Channah approached the group of men and sat on the soft grass.

"Alexander has something to tell you," Avram said.

Alexander fidgeted with the hem of his tunic. "Two weeks ago, Thalia. Well, let me start over." He looked toward his father, who nodded. "I have been holding payment for the matchmaker Thalia to find John Simon's wife and family."

Channah could not help interrupting. "John Simon? My husband?"

"Well, yes, but I just found that out," Alexander said. "You see, he came to Ephesus looking for you."

"I knew it."

“He paid Thalia to let me know when you got here. To Ephesus, I mean. So, about two weeks ago, she came and asked me to pay her the money. She knew things John Simon told me, details she could not be aware of without speaking with someone from your family. And so, I paid her and sent a message to my cousin in Laodicea to tell John Simon to come back.” Alexander licked his lips. “But I have not heard from Eli. That is my cousin. So, I have no way to know if he received my message or if John Simon was already gone from Laodicea or if he never got there, or what.”

“But he is alive.” Channah could feel her heart fluttering. “Thank God.”

“Yes. So, anyway, after I paid her Thalia said she had found me a wife. A week later, my father paid her for making me a match. When we looked at the map of where to find Rebecca, I realized it was the same map that I sent to John Simon. Well, really, the map I sent my cousin.”

Zimri spoke up. “The coincidence was beyond belief. I was concerned that Thalia was up to something sly. She has a reputation of being very shrewd when it comes to making money. So, my family talked it over.” He glanced toward his son. “Alexander had some reservations about speaking of this matter, since you have asked Thalia to find a match for you.”

Channah interrupted, “But I have not--,”

“I did. Without your knowledge,” Avram confessed. “Forgive me. I only did what I thought best for you and the children.”

Zimri continued, “I decided we should question all of you, separately, to learn more information.” He held out his hands, palms up. “And now we see for certain that you are the same woman John Simon is searching for.”

“Where is Laodicea?” Channah asked.

“Quite some distance away,” Zimri replied. “I wish I could give you some assurance your husband will return to Ephesus, but we truly have no way to know.”

Channah tried to remain calm. “I am grateful to know he did not perish in the shipwreck off Joppa. How long it will take, I cannot guess. But I know John Simon will come home to us.”

“He left a bag of coins for you.” Alexander held out a leather pouch.

Channah accepted it, wiped a tear, and tucked the bag into her sash. “Thank you.”

When Avram stood, everyone else got to their feet as well. “Now,” he said, “Let us break bread together and plan Alexander and Rebecca’s wedding celebration.”

Chapter Forty-Three

John Simon limped into the city. Following his well-established pattern, he stopped the first man he encountered and asked in Greek where he could find the synagogue.

The merchant stopped pushing his vegetable cart. "What is a synagogue?"

"A house of worship. Perhaps you can tell me where the Jews live in this city."

"Oh. You must be looking for the Kerateion. It is south." He waved. "That way, near the old city wall. How about a nice, fresh head of cabbage? I harvested them myself, this very morning."

"No thank you, but I do appreciate the directions."

The man shrugged and wheeled his cart on down the street.

John Simon periodically checked the sun's position, to make certain he kept moving in a southerly direction.

It was a long time before he began to see homes with mezuzahs affixed to their doorposts. The soles of his feet ached from walking the last hundred miles barefoot after his sandals fell apart. "Excuse me." He addressed an old woman with a water pot on her head. "Would you be so kind as to direct me to the synagogue?"

"It is not far." The woman set her water pot on the ground and looked him up and down. "If you are a beggar, no one at the synagogue will help you. There is a cave near the river where the dissidents meet. You would be more likely to get a handout from them."

John Simon felt a jolt of excitement. "Are they followers of the Way?"

"No. I mean the Christians. Follow this road all the way to the city gate. Ask anyone where to find the large grotto where people meet on the first day of the week." She picked up her water pot. "Shalom."

"Shalom." John Simon sat on a stoop and rubbed his tired feet before continuing down the road. "Christians," he said aloud. "That is a novel name."

The sun was low in the sky when he found a large cave near the river. The trampled vegetation around the mouth of the cave told him a crowd had been here. However, the area was deserted this evening.

By his calculations, tomorrow was the first day of the week. If he was at the right place, there should be a gathering of believers here in the morning. If not, he at least had shelter for the evening. He sat just inside the mouth of the cave and opened his knapsack.

John Simon awoke before sunrise. He stood and stretched his arms. As soon as the sky began to lighten, he went outside and sat on the damp grass. Always a man of habit, he recited a Psalm, said his morning prayer of thanksgiving, and meditated on words he heard Jesus speak on the mountain years ago. Then he prayed earnestly for Channah, Miriam, and Avram.

A voice sounded from behind John Simon. "Shalom." He turned to see a man about his own age with pale skin, black hair, bushy eyebrows, and exceptionally dark eyes. "Are you here for the meeting?"

"If your gathering is to worship Jesus, I will be most happy to join in before I continue my journey. My name is John Simon."

The man smiled. "I am Joseph, but everyone calls me Barnabas." He sat on the grass, next to John Simon.

"Barnabas? That means 'son of encouragement' does it not?

“Yes. I strive to live up to that name.”

“I could use some encouragement right now.” John Simon rubbed his left foot. “My family and I fled Bethlehem five years ago, but we were shipwrecked and separated. I do not know for certain that they are still alive.” He shifted and massaged his right foot. “We were bound for Ephesus. They were not there when I was finally able to get to the city. So, I am walking along the Via Maris to Israel, praying to meet my family coming this way. We are shepherds. My wife’s name is Channah. She is traveling with her elderly Uncle Avram and our daughter Miriam, who is practically a young lady by now. Have you seen or heard of them by any chance?”

“No,” Barnabas answered. “But I have just recently arrived here from Cyprus. Do not lose heart, my brother. With God, nothing is impossible.”

“Thank you. I see how you earned your nickname. Oddly enough, I spent a brief time on Cyprus, after the shipwreck. The people there were very kind.”

“We Cypriots are known for our hospitality. Come with me after the morning worship. My family is living in a stable not far from here while our house Is being built. My wife will feed you well, and you are welcome to lodge in the other end of our stable until you are ready to continue your journey.”

“Thank you. It would be good to give my sore feet a few days of rest.”

“Ah, here comes my friend Lucius.” Barnabas jumped to his feet. “Lucius relocated to Antioch from Cyrene some time ago.”

John Simon stood to greet the new arrivals. Barnabas introduced him to Lucius and his family.

“My new friend John Simon is searching for his wife. What is her name? Hannah?”

“Channah, a shepherdess. She is with our child Miriam and her very old uncle.”

“We had a Channah here, but she was a weaver,” Lucius’s wife said. “I forget her daughter’s name. I do recall she was traveling with an old gentleman named Avram.”

“Yes.” John Simon felt the hair on the back of his neck tingle as if lightning was in the air. “Avram is my wife’s uncle’s name. Channah was here in Antioch?”

Lucius pursed his lips. “We have seen many refugees come through the city. Sometimes I get them confused. It seems to me the weaver’s husband died and that is why she had to remain here for a while.”

“No,” his wife said. “That was the other woman. The one named Rebecca. Channah had the little boy named Joshua, like our eldest. They were on their way to Ephesus, I believe.”

John Simon picked up his bag and dusted grass from the back of his tunic. “A boy? How old?”

“I am not certain. Three or four I would guess.” The woman peered into the cave. “Eliana would know for sure, but she has not yet arrived this morning.” She put a hand to her head. “Now that I think about it, there *was* a girl named Miriam with them. She was a sweet child, so devoted to her little brother.”

“Much as I would love to worship with you this morning, I cannot think about anything other than getting on a ship to Ephesus. Can you direct me to the harbor?”

Lucius smiled. “My son will take you there in our cart.”

As John Simon climbed into the cart, Barnabas caught his arm. “Are you able to pay your passage?”

“I always think of myself as a shepherd, but I have enough experience working on ships to get a job as a sailor. At this moment, I feel as if I could swim to Ephesus."

Barnabas's parting words were, "God be with you, my brother. I will pray for you to be reunited with your family."

Chapter Forty-Four

"I have a son," John Simon told the sailor next to him as they loaded spices.

"I have four boys myself. Well, perhaps only three are really mine. The numbers do not add up for the birth of the fourth one." He pushed an amphora of oil to the side. "Claudia said he was born early, even though he was a big, strong baby, I did not press her. You know how lonely sailors' wives can get."

John Simon pondered the sailor's words as he worked up a heavy sweat. Perhaps Channah had taken another husband. After all, they had not seen each other for years. She had no way of knowing if he was dead or alive. She seemed so certain she was barren. Maybe she married a man who had been widowed and brought a son with him. Perhaps he should have waited in Antioch to gather more information. It was too late for second thoughts now. He was on a fast ship whose next port was Ephesus. After a great deal of thought, he resolved to approach Channah without letting her know his identity. If she had found happiness with someone else, he planned to disappear without letting her know he was alive.

That night, he lay awake on the ship's deck, unable to sleep. He put his hands under his head and stared up at the stars. Those same lights were shining down on his wife. But was she his? He was glad Barnabas promised to pray for him, since he did not know what to ask God to do. With all his heart, he wanted to be the one who shared Channah's laughter and even her tears for the rest of their lives. Yet he forced himself to intercede for Channah to have whatever was best for her.

If Channah did indeed have a son but no husband, John Simon hoped he could learn to be a good abba to the boy, as he believed he had with Miriam. His little girl, the apple of his eye. How much of her growing up had he missed in going on five years?

The voyage to Ephesus seemed to take forever, although in truth it lasted only a few days. When John Simon spoke of Jesus, the sailors seemed uninterested. The moment he saw the temple of Artemis looming in the distance, he gathered his few possessions. He could be done with his work and in the heart of the city soon.

A morning shower left the marble on Ephesus's main thoroughfare extremely slick. John Simon hurried to help a man who slipped and sprawled in front of him, sending loaves of bread flying in every direction. With John Simon's assistance the man was able to stand. He gathered the loaves, tucked them back into his broken basket, and went on his way without so much as a thank you.

Despite wanting to get on with his mission, John Simon stopped to purchase a plain tunic and new sandals. Before putting them on, he went to a public bath and washed his body. It felt good to be cleansed of the ship's salty grime. He put his old tunic in the bottom of his knapsack. Fabric was too precious to throw away, even when a garment was worn beyond patching. After washing, the old tunic would make a good drying rag. He considering shaving, but decided against it. Channah was less likely to recognize him behind his bushy beard.

He had spent almost five years searching for his family. Now that he was on the threshold of seeing them, it took all the courage he could summon to continue. He made his way to Alexander's home. If Channah was in Ephesus, Thalia the matchmaker was sure to waste no time collecting the fee John Simon left in Alexander's keeping.

Feeling weak with anticipation, he knocked at the door. No answer. He had not come this far only to be thwarted in his quest. He began to pound on the door, shouting, "Alexander. It is John Simon. Open up."

From across the narrow street, a neighbor shouted from his second-story rooftop, "Stop making so much noise. Alexander is getting married today, and the whole family has gone to celebrate."

John Simon turned around. "Where is the wedding?"

"How would I know? I was not invited."

John Simon leaned against the door, totally frustrated. Drawing a deep breath, he realized Thalia was his only recourse unless he wanted to wait for Alexander to return. He hitched up his belt and made short work of the walk to the matchmaker's house.

Thalia opened her door and stared at John Simon. "You have been here before." She cocked her head to one side. "Without the beard."

"You have a good memory. I am John Simon, and I am still searching for my wife Channah."

With a raised eyebrow, Thalia motioned for him to enter the house. "Do come in."

She led him to her writing table. "What may I do for you?"

"I am pretty sure my family is here in Ephesus."

Thalia's eyes were on a stack of papyrus sheets. "What led you to that conclusion?"

"When I got to Antioch, I spoke with people who told me Channah and a group of believers had been there. They left on a ship bound for Ephesus." He hunched forward, resting his elbows on her table. "Have you heard they are here?"

The matchmaker shuffled a papyrus leaf from the bottom of the stack in front of her, and seemed to be reading it. "I believe our agreement was that I am to provide information about, let me see. Ah, yes, Channah,

Avram, and Miriam. If I should happen to learn their whereabouts, I am to give that information to Alexander, the ferry rowboat operator." She made eye contact with John Simon. "Have you spoken with Alexander?"

"No. There is no one home at his house."

"I see." Thalia pressed her lips together. "No doubt that is not a permanent situation." She broke into a warm smile. "However, you strike me as a man who does not like to wait."

"More than one person has told me I am impatient," he confessed. "Or impulsive. Perhaps that is the same thing."

"Suppose I were to go through my records and search for a family that fits the description of the people you seek. What are you willing to pay for my time and effort?"

"I have already made provisions for payment through Alexander."

"So you have," Thalia agreed. "And I have met the terms of our contract by delivering the required information to Alexander." She held up a thin, neatly-cut leaf. "This is the new thing. It is called parchment. They say it lasts longer than papyrus, but it is quite costly."

John Simon took out the smallest denomination coin he had and placed it between himself and Thalia.

She glanced at it and folded her arms. "The people you seek arrived in Ephesus."

"Where can I find them?"

The matchmaker shrugged. "Answering that question requires research."

"How much for the research?"

"Because I like you, and because I really want you to see your wife today, five of those." She nodded toward the coin.

John Simon took four additional coins and slammed them onto the table, glaring at Thalia.

She smiled and picked up the money. Then she withdrew a sheet from the bottom of her stack. "I happen to have come across a copy of a map—"

John Simon snatched it from her hand and began to study it. "This is not a map of Ephesus."

"No. Shepherds live with sheep, and sheep do not usually dwell in big cities. Go and cross the river. You will see the path where the map picks up." She leaned back in her chair and put one hand behind her neck. "For a fee, I will arrange for someone to guide you."

"If I can navigate the great sea by the stars, I am certain I can find a pasture with a map." He stood, picked up his knapsack, and left.

"You are welcome," he heard Thalia call after him.

Chapter Forty-Five

John Simon's irritation at the matchmaker's shrewd ways melted as he made his way to the river crossing. "Where is Alexander?" he asked the fellow manning the rowboat's oars.

"He got married this morning. I do not expect him back at work until next week."

John Simon settled into the boat and reviewed the map.

"Are you lost?" the ferryman asked.

"Not exactly. I am going somewhere I have not been before, the pasture belonging to Ali Allisad.

"Ah." The rower rested his arms on the oars. "Just follow the pathway from the ferry landing. It will take you right by the place you want."

"Thank you. Approximately how far is it to the Ali Allisad pasture?"

"Walking rapidly, about a half hour."

Despite sore feet and new sandals, John Simon set a quick pace. Nearing the crest of what he hoped was the last hill, he heard an unusual noise. He stopped and listened. The buzz of a crowd? Sprinkled with laughter? These were strange noises to come from a pasture. Puzzled, he advanced slowly.

At the hilltop, he paused to survey the scene in the meadow. John Simon was confused. That scoundrel Thalia must have given him directions to Alexander's wedding party instead of telling him where to find Channah.

He progressed down the hill, remaining on the path. From his vantage point, he recognized Alexander by the patch over his eye. He was dancing in a circle of men.

"Are you a friend of the bride or the groom?" a man standing near the pathway asked.

"I am acquainted with Alexander, but I was not invited to the wedding. I just arrived back in Ephesus this morning."

"Come on over and enjoy some food and drink anyway."

John Simon suspected the man had consumed a little too much wine, a common occurrence at weddings. Since he had eaten very little since the previous evening, the choice delicacies served at weddings sounded most appealing. "I do not want to intrude on your celebration."

"Nonsense. There is plenty. I am Alexander's cousin Eli. I came all the way from Laodicea for this auspicious occasion. What is your name?"

"I am John Simon. I met Alexander—"

Eli grabbed his arm and interrupted. "John Simon? The John Simon Alexander wrote about to me?"

"I do not know about any writing—"

Eli embraced him. "I told him you never came to Laodicea. We were concerned something happened to you on the way."

"During my travels, I went to the synagogue in Laodicea. The rabbi told me there were no followers of the Way in his city. I did not believe him, but I could not find where you gathered. After two days of searching, I moved on to the next town."

"I must go and tell Alexander you are here. He will be delighted. Meanwhile, have something to eat."

John Simon went immediately to the food. His first selection was a small loaf of bread, the size and shape Channah used to make for him. At his first bite, a little boy tugged on his tunic.

"Are you my abba?" the lad asked.

John Simon swallowed the bread in his mouth. Then he knelt and studied the boy. Except for being younger and smaller, the face he saw before him belonged to his own father. "What is your name?"

Without a trace of shyness, the boy replied, "Joshua."

"How old are you, Joshua?" John Simon asked with mounting excitement.

He held up four fingers. "Four, but I will be five pretty soon."

John Simon bowed his head, struggling to control his emotions. He saw a woman's skirt appear behind Joshua.

"You are not bothering this gentleman, are you?"

The sound of his wife's voice fell around John Simon like a welcome summer rain. His plan to conceal his identity abandoned him. He scooped Joshua into his arms as he sprang to his feet. "Yes, son." He kissed the boy. "In answer to your question, I *am* your abba."

"John Simon," Channah whispered. "It is you."

"Yes." Still holding Joshua, he embraced Channah with his other arm. "Yes, my darling. It is I."

"We found my abba," Joshua shouted. "My abba is home."

"Where is Miriam?" John Simon asked.

"She is with Uncle Avram and the sheep in the far pasture. We knew the crowd would frighten the animals." She removed her apron and used it to wipe tears. "Joshua and I will take you there." She inclined her head against his chest. "Oh, John Simon, I am so happy you have come home." She motioned to a woman standing nearby. "Please take over serving the wine." She turned her smile back toward him. "I am going to the far pasture with my husband."

John Simon stood Joshua on the ground and grabbed two more loaves of bread. He and Channah walked hand in hand, while their son skipped ahead.

As soon as they crossed over a small rise, John Simon glanced behind to make sure they were out of the crowd's sight. Then he caught Channah into his embrace and kissed her.

She eagerly responded. After more kisses, she said, "Oh, John Simon, I have missed you more than words can ever say. So many people tried to convince me to pronounce you dead, but I never gave up hope."

"I had many close calls. But every time circumstances became impossible, God sent someone to help me."

"I know what you mean. If a believer named Dorcas had not taken me in, I would probably still be in Joppa trying to earn passage money. I was separated from Uncle Avram and Miriam in the shipwreck. The two of them spent months on a deserted island, but in the end God brought them home to me."

"We have many stories to share. I prayed for all of you often."

"As I did for you every day." They walked on in silence for a while. "Uncle is not himself these days. His health is failing."

"Ima. Abba. Hurry," Joshua ran toward them. "I told Miriam and Grandfather you are coming. They do not believe me."

"We will be there soon," Channah replied, laughing and crying at the same time. "That boy is so like you."

Chapter Forty-Six

Some weeks later, Channah was rubbing oil on a lamb's ears when she saw Miriam walking purposefully toward her, moving as fast as she could without frightening the sheep. "Ima," the girl said breathlessly, "Abba says to come quickly. Grandfather fainted."

"Help Rebecca finish the oiling." She handed the flask to Miriam and went to the tent where Avram now spent most of his days. John Simon was there, kneeling beside the thick fleece where her uncle lay.

"What happened?" she whispered.

"I am not certain." John Simon laid a blanket over Avram's feet. I found him lying on the ground."

Not knowing what else to do, Channah wet a rag with wine and dabbed at her uncle's forehead. "He has fever."

John Simon massaged Avram's hand. "Do you know of the growth on his stomach?"

"No." Channah was surprised. "He has not spoken of any such thing."

John Simon drew the blanket up to Avram's waist. Then he reached underneath and pulled the old man's tunic up to reveal a lump the size of a melon protruding from his abdomen.

Channah gasped. "Shall I send Rebecca to fetch a physician?"

Avram's eyelids fluttered. "It is too late for doctors They cannot do anything for me."

"But Uncle."

"But what?" Avram's voice grew stronger. "A physician will only poke and prod and ask for money and then say he cannot help. Just comfort me as you would a ewe trying to deliver her lamb. Let me die in peace, here in the fields where the sheep graze, with the family I love."

John Simon filled a cup and lifted Avram's head. "Will you take wine?"

"Yes." Avram drained the cup before John Simon returned him to a prone position. "Wine helps with the pain. Thank you, my son."

Channah mopped his brow again. "You cannot die."

Avram closed his eyes. "It is time. Perhaps not today, but soon. Very soon." He reached for Channah's hand. "Do not grieve for me, little one."

"There must be something I can do," she said.

"You have already done it." He squeezed her hand. "You brought more joy to your Auntie and me than you will ever know." He closed his eyes and smiled. "Or perhaps you do know, because of Miriam and the boy."

"You should rest," John Simon said. "Talking seems to wear you out."

Avram ignored the admonition. "John Simon, you have been like a son to me. I am inspired by your faith. I could not be leaving Channah in better hands. Take good care of her.

"I promise." John Simon wiped at tears. "Thank you for entrusting her to me."

"May I see my grandchildren? And Rebecca?"

"I will get them." John Simon kissed Avram's cheek, hugged Channah, and exited the tent.

Soon Rebecca came inside, wiping her hands. "Oh, Father. What will we do without you?

"You will be fine." He raised a hand and touched her cheek. "Trust in the Lord and follow His ways all of your life."

Rebecca laid her cheek on his. "Thank you for taking me into your family. Thank you for finding me a good husband." She dissolved into choking sobs.

"I am proud to call you my daughter."

Miriam, Julia, and Joshua filed quietly into the tent with sober faces.

"Why so solemn, my grandchildren? Come and hug your old grandfather."

"Julia," Avram said. "Always remember that you are greatly loved. Learn everything you can about Jesus, and he will sustain you."

"I will, Grandfather." She stepped forward and kissed Avram's cheek.

"Joshua." He beckoned to the boy. "You can do nothing better than to grow up be a man like your abba. He will teach you the Way, and you must follow it faithfully."

"Yes, Grandfather."

"Now kiss me goodbye."

The boy did as he was told.

"Miriam, little one," Avram's voice broke.

She buried her face in his neck. "Do not leave me," she begged.

Avram caressed her head. "Do you remember the lesson about David and his infant son? It is the same with us. I must go, but someday you will come to me. First, I want you to have a long and happy life of faith and love."

She sat on the side of his fleecy bed. "But I have not yet finished learning all of the Psalms."

"Your abba will teach you. Right now, let us recite the shepherd psalm."

Miriam sat straight and began, "The Lord is my shepherd. I shall not want."

Avram joined in. "He maketh me to lie down in green pastures. He leadeth me beside the still waters…"

Rebecca and Channah spoke in unison with them at "Yea, though I walk through the valley of the shadow of death, I will fear no evil for thou art with me" through the end of the Psalm.

Avram was clearly struggling for breath. "You see, little one, a shadow cannot hurt anyone. And we only see shadows when there is a great light casting them. Do you understand?"

"No, Grandfather."

"You will someday. I will sleep now."

When Avram closed his eyes, Rebecca took Julia by the hand. "Come children. You can help me prepare the evening meal."

Channah started to rise, but Rebecca put a staying hand on her shoulder. "You should stay with him. You are his heart."

From time to time, Avram roused. He drank more wine, but refused to take food. "It will only come back up," he murmured. Occasionally, he mumbled a few words and then went back to sleep.

Long after dark, he opened his eyes. "You should go to bed," he told Channah, who still sat at his bedside.

"I cannot leave you. Please do not ask me to."

"What do you suppose Heaven is like?"

"I do not know."

"No. No one does." After a pause, he added, "According to the prophet, it is beyond anything the mind of man can conceive of. Think of it. Soon, with clear eyes, this ignorant old shepherd will see God face to face."

"You are not ignorant. You are the wisest man I have ever known."

He grunted. "I saw him once, when he was wrapped in flesh and walked on this earth."

"Yes, Uncle, you have told me that story many times."

He slept for a while. Unexpectedly, he began to speak again. "We had some good times, you and Yael and me."

"Yes, we did," she replied.

"In the springtime, when the hills are covered with wildflowers and the new lambs are frisking about with the sheer delight of being alive, think of those times and remember me."

"I will think of you every day. I love you."

"Ah, sweet Channah, I love you, too. Do not live your life looking backward, though. Press forward into the future, with a song on your lips, love in your heart, and the hope of Jesus in your spirit."

He lifted his arms. "Ah, you are here. I knew you would come for me."

After a moment, his arms dropped and his head lolled to the side. Channah knew he was dead, even before she felt for the stopped heartbeat. She kissed her uncle one last time and stepped outside into the starry night.

Channah turned at the sound of footsteps. "I was coming to check on you." John Simon slipped a shawl over her shoulders. "I thought you might need this."

“He is gone.” She leaned against her husband’s muscular chest and cried.

“He was a good man.” John Simon held her close to him. “Let the tears flow. You need to release them.”

Chapter Forty-Seven

The next morning, Channah felt numb as she and Rebecca set out the family breakfast. “Our father will rest in Alexander’s family tomb,” Rebecca said. “John Simon has gone to the city to get the spices we need to prepare the body.”

Channah nodded. “Good. Thank you.”

The children were subdued during the meal, but soon afterward Julia and Joshua were laughing and playing tag. Miriam quietly tended the sheep.

When Channah repeated Avram’s last words to Rebecca, her adopted sister asked, “Who do you suppose he was talking to at the end?”

“Someone he was expecting. Maybe an angel. Perhaps the Lord himself.” Channah began putting dishes away. “If we were supposed to know, my eyes would have been opened just as Uncle’s were.”

“Yes,” Channah continued. “I believe the vision was for him alone.” She glanced at the brightening sunrise. “Everything is so normal. The sun is up. The grass is blowing in the breeze. The sheep are ready to graze.”

Rebecca looked puzzled. “So?”

“It just seems as if there should be some acknowledgement that a wonderful man is no longer with us.” Channah shrugged. “I am not making sense.”

“You are tired. And grieving.”

“Yes. Maybe that is why I feel so peculiar. I will go to the pasture now. Miriam needs help with the sheep.”

She took an unexplained comfort from the nearness of the animals. As the days went by, the love of her husband and children, along with Rebecca’s agreeable companionship helped the dazed feeling ebb away.

One morning, she noticed an odd scent in the air. She was so accustomed to the smells associated with sheep that she hardly noticed them anymore. This was something different, and rather foul. Whatever it was went away, but the next morning, she noticed it again. Something nasty, like stagnant seawater.

On the third day, the unpleasant smell brought a wave of nausea with it. Channah counted the days since her last time of bleeding. *I am with child.* When the symptoms continued for another week, she was sure.

"You are in a good mood today." John Simon pecked her cheek before they led the sheep to a fresh pasture.

"I have much to be thankful for." Channah said. Making sure Miriam was out of earshot, she added. "And so do you."

"I could not agree more. We are extraordinarily blessed. We can worship Jesus as we please, our family is well provided for, our children are healthy, and my wife bakes bread as light as air. What more could a man ask for?"

"Is there nothing at all you wish for?" she asked.

"I can think of nothing." After a moment, he said, "It would be nice to have our own herd again, instead of tending someone else's sheep. Is that what you mean?"

They walked on for a while. Then he asked, "Are *you* longing for something?"

"I am."

With a look of surprise, he stopped and turned to her. "What do you want? Because whatever it is, I will do my best to obtain it."

"You have already done your part." Channah walked on. "Now it is up to me to finish the work."

He caught up to her. "My part of what? I do not understand what you mean."

"It is somewhat like baking bread. You have put the yeast into the dough. Now, all I must do is wait for the loaf to rise."

"What are you talking about?"

Channah stopped walking and took his hand. "I am expecting a child."

John Simon let out a whoop that sent sheep scattering. "Oh, Channah. This is wonderful news. The children will be so excited, too. When shall we tell them?"

"Now is fine as far as I am concerned."

John Simon motioned for Miriam to come near.

"Did you step on a thorn, abba?" she asked. "I heard a yelp."

"No." His lopsided grin stretched across his face. "Your ima has something to tell you. Something wonderful."

"I am going to have a baby," Channah said.

Miriam covered her mouth, but not securely enough to prevent the escape of a high-pitched squeal. She bounced up and down on the balls of her feet. "When?"

Channah laughed aloud. "In six or seven months."

"Oh, ima, how wonderful. It has to be a girl, because I already have a brother. Now I need a sister.

"We will not know that until the child Is born," Channah said.

"May I go and tell Rebecca and Joshua?"

Channah and John Simon exchanged glances. “Why not?” he asked.

“All right.” Channah reached to caress her daughter, but Miriam was already running back to the tents.

Chapter Forty-Eight

"Have one of the security guards escort you to the market," Dorcas instructed Salome. She held out a coin. "This is all I can afford to spend today."

Salome took the coin and inspected it. "Enough for a head of cabbage I suppose."

"That sounds fine to me." Dorcas smiled. "I will bake bread to go with it. My loaves never turn out as well as Channah's did, but they will suffice."

"Ah, Channah. I still miss her and little Joshua."

"So do I." Dorcas closed her coin box and returned it to the shelf behind her. "It would please me greatly to know she and her family are living safely in Ephesus, and that she has been reunited with her husband. And that Julia is thriving."

"No doubt they are all well." Salome assured her. After a moment of silence, she asked, "How much longer do you plan to keep the shop closed?"

Dorcas shrugged. "Until the trouble passes."

"Let us hope that day comes soon." Salome tucked the coin into her belt. "Surely you realize the religious leaders want to stop you from telling your story of being raised from the dead."

"Perhaps. Nevertheless, as long as I have breath in my body, I will continue to speak of what the Lord has done for me. He will provide."

"I never thought things would come to this in Joppa." Salome shook her head. "After so many incidents, the refugees no longer go to the camp. Widows who follow the Way fear to leave their houses. I must confess, at night I jump at the slightest noise myself."

"God's providence is in all that happens. For example, now that the travelers no longer use the camp, I am considering an offer to sell that pasture."

"No, Dorcas. That piece of land and the well next to it belonged to Captain Joseph's grandfather. How can you think of letting it go?"

"When the choice is between owning land or eating, the decision becomes very simple."

Salome put a hand to her mouth. "Surely things are not that desperate."

"Not quite, not yet." Dorcas smoothed her tunic. "While you are at the market, I am going to take clothing to the ship I saw approaching the harbor."

"I would try to convince you not to go, but I know I would be wasting words." Salome removed her apron. "I must say, however, that with us eating cabbage soup every other day, the Lord surely knows you have nothing to spare for shipwrecked sailors."

"Remember Peter telling us Jesus's words? That if we have two coats, we are to give one away?"

Salome grunted. "I trust you at least have the good sense to take a bodyguard with you."

Ignoring Salome's warning, Dorcas gathered four plain tunics and made her way alone down the steep pathway from her house to the sea. She enjoyed praying on this path, and did not want a bodyguard along to intrude on her time with God. Her prayers this particular morning focused on Channah and Julia. *Did I make a mistake, sending my fair-haired baby girl away with a couple I barely know?*

At the dock, she spoke with a sailor, who told her the captain picked up a fellow seaman in Alexandria.

Dorcas handed the sailor a tunic. "He may need this."

“I suspect he does. He was wearing a rag as a breech cloth last time I saw him.”

She stood thinking of the many ships she had met over the years. Most of the time, she never saw the recipients of her generosity again. But there were special encounters when she met Salome, and Channah, and Sophia. She remembered the day Avram and Miriam came home to Channah. Perhaps someday, she would see her husband’s ship come sailing into the harbor. She sighed. Perhaps. Some day.

“Dorcas.”

Startled, she turned to see a man dressed in the tunic she gave the sailor a short while ago. “Joseph.” She stepped toward him, reminding herself it was improper for a woman to take hold of a man in public, even if he was her husband.

Joseph was not so restrained. He wrapped her in a hug. “Oh, my sweet gazelle. How I have missed you.”

“Joseph, you are so thin. What happened? I expected you would come home more than a year ago.”

“Pirates,” he said. “They seized my ship west of Malta. My crew and I were sold as slaves. Have you seen any of my men?”

“None that I am aware of.” Dorcas snuggled against his chest. “Are you strong enough to walk up the hill?”

“Yes.” He released his hold on her. “You cannot imagine how many times I dreamed of climbing that cliff again with you by my side.”

As they made their leisurely way toward their house, Dorcas told her husband of the events in Joppa over the past five years.

“Persecution is driving many followers of the Way away from our homeland,” Joseph told her. “There are quite a few believers living in the Jewish community in Alexandria. I would not have escaped from slavery without their help."

"Praise God you are home. Your ship is gone and my business has dried up. Nevertheless, we have each other and our faith in Jesus."

Joseph smiled at her. "By my reckoning, we are the wealthiest couple in Joppa."

THE END

Discussion Questions

Why do you think Saul of Tarsus was so hostile toward the followers of Jesus?

Do you agree with John Simon that the persecution of early Christians in Israel had more to do with power than truth?

How do you feel about Dorcas's decision to give up Julia? Should she have kept the baby in Joppa?

What convinced Salome to overcome her objection to the gentile baby in Dorcas's household?

Do you think Cornelius may have been the same Roman centurion who later became a Christian? (Acts, Chapter 10)

Why didn't Rebecca choose to remain in Antioch?

What did you think of Thalia the Matchmaker?

Why was Avram determined to find husbands for Channah and Rebeca?

Why didn't John Simon want Channah to recognize him right away?

Can you think of any good that came from the shepherd family's separation?

Other Books

BY CARLENE HAVEL & SHARON FAUCHEUX

Song of the Shepherd Woman

The Scarlet Cord

Daughter of the King

BY CARLENE HAVEL

A Hero's Homecoming

Baxter Road Miracle

Evidence Not Seen

Parisian Surprise

A Sharecropper Christmas

Texas Runaway Bride

The Twice-Shy Heart

20th Century Man

2Sweet 2Be 4Gotten

BY BILLIE HOUSTON & CARLENE HAVEL

Discovering Emily

Old Maid Bride

Lucky in Love

That Scott Woman

Made in the USA
Monee, IL
18 September 2023